Enrollment Form

☐ *Yes!* I WANT TO BE A *P*RIVILEGED *W*OMAN.

Enclosed is one *PAGES & PRIVILEGES*™ Proof of Purchase from any Harlequin or Silhouette book currently for sale in stores (Proofs of Purchase are found on the back pages of books) and the store cash register receipt. Please enroll me in *PAGES & PRIVILEGES*™. Send my Welcome Kit and FREE Gifts -- and activate my FREE benefits -- immediately.

More great gifts and benefits to come like these luxurious Truly Lace and L'Effleur gift baskets.

▼ DETACH HERE AND MAIL TODAY! ▼

NAME (please print)
_____

ADDRESS _____ APT. NO _____

CITY _____ STATE _____ ZIP/POSTAL CODE _____

☐ **Pages & Privileges™** SAMPLE ONLY **PROOF OF PURCHASE**

Please allow 6-8 weeks for delivery. Quantities are limited. We reserve the right to substitute items. Enroll before October 31, 1995 and receive one full year of benefits.

NO CLUB! NO COMMITMENT!
Just one purchase brings you great **Free Gifts** and **Benefits!**
(More details in back of this book.)

Name of store where this book was purchased_____

Date of purchase_____

Type of store:

☐ Bookstore ☐ Supermarket ☐ Drugstore

☐ Dept. or discount store (e.g. K-Mart or Walmart)

☐ Other (specify)_____

Which Harlequin or Silhouette series do you usually read?

Complete and mail with one Proof of Purchase and store receipt to:

U.S.: *PAGES & PRIVILEGES*™, P.O. Box 1960, Danbury, CT 06813-1960

Canada: *PAGES & PRIVILEGES*™, 49-6A The Donway West, P.O. 813, North York, ON M3C 2E8   **PRINTED IN U.S.A**

Nothing About This Situation Was Normal.

Knowing she had to meet Bronson's gaze sooner or later, Tamara steeled herself. His eyes held gentle knowledge, and his smile was rueful.

"You're not sure if this was a good idea after all," he told her, his smooth baritone washing over her skin like a feather, both delicate and unsettling.

Meeting both his gaze and her own feelings head-on, she nodded. "This doesn't feel right."

"Because you feel we're betraying our kids?"

"In a way. We're telling them they cannot feel a certain way—"

"And here we are, experiencing the same emotions."

Dear Reader,

Here at Desire, hot summer months mean even *hotter* reading, beginning with Joan Johnston's *The Disobedient Bride*, the next addition to her fabulous Children of Hawk's Way series—*and* July's *Man of the Month*.

Next up is *Falcon's Lair*, a sizzling love story by Sara Orwig, an author many of you already know—although she's new to Desire. And if you like family stories, don't miss Christine Rimmer's unforgettable *Cat's Cradle or* Caroline Cross's delightful *Operation Mommy*.

A book from award winner Helen R. Myers is always a treat, so I'm glad we have *The Rebel and the Hero* this month. And Diana Mars's many fans will be thrilled with *Mixed-up Matrimony*. If you like humor, you'll like this engaging—and *very* sensuous—love story.

Next month, there is much more to look forward to, including *The Wilde Bunch*, a *Man of the Month* by Barbara Boswell, and *Heart of the Hunter*, the first book in a new series by BJ James.

As always, your opinions are important to me. So continue to let me know what you like about Silhouette Desire!

Sincerely,

Lucia Macro
Senior Editor

Please address questions and book requests to:
Silhouette Reader Service
U.S.: 3010 Walden Ave., P.O. Box 1325, Buffalo, NY 14269
Canadian: P.O. Box 609, Fort Erie, Ont. L2A 5X3

DIANA
MARS
MIXED-UP MATRIMONY

SILHOUETTE *Desire*®
Published by Silhouette Books
America's Publisher of Contemporary Romance

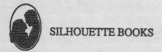

SILHOUETTE BOOKS

ISBN 0-373-05942-6

MIXED-UP MATRIMONY

Copyright © 1995 by Deanna Marliss

Printed in U.S.A.

Books by Diana Mars

Silhouette Desire

Peril in Paradise #906
Mixed-Up Matrimony #942

DIANA MARS

feels fortunate to be a part of the Golden Age of Romance, which has seen so many exciting elements added: suspense, horror, mystery, the supernatural. Although she has worked in the fields of business, languages and anthropology, writing has proven to be the strongest, yet most satisfying, challenge.

To Cory, with love:
May all the decisions you make in life
fulfill all your dreams.

One

Notre Dame's famed Golden Dome loomed straight ahead, gleaming under the rays of an autumn sun.

Bronson Kensington looked at it with mounting frustration. Ever since he'd received the call from Brandy Cavanaugh, his cousin and head tennis coach at Deerbrook High, fury at his only child had mounted.

How *dare* he? How could Christopher have done this to him? Even dared consider it?

As Bronson drove around the Courtney Tennis Center—the impressive Irish outdoor facility—he bitterly reflected that he would have loved having the opportunity to attend a school with the tradition, name-recognition and academic excellence that this South Bend university boasted.

Unlike his wealthy cousin, Bronson had been forced to settle for two years at a community college, after which he'd been able to transfer to Central Illinois College. He'd learned the hard way that top jobs were acquired through connections.

For his son, his pride and joy, Bronson wished the world. He wanted Christopher's college years to be worry free, a golden time in his life he could look back on fondly.

As Bronson searched for a racy red Toyota Celica, he rocked his lower jaw from side to side. It was sore and stiff from his nervous grinding of teeth ever since he'd gotten the phone call from Brandy earlier in the day....

"Bronson, sorry to bother you at work—" she'd begun.

"What is it, Brandy?" Bronson had asked, alarmed. Although he and his cousin were close, their busy schedules meant they seldom had time to see each other, and Brandy would not call unless it was something urgent. "Christopher! Is he hurt? Was he in an accident? Did he—?"

"Hold on, hold on, Bronson," Brandy Cavanaugh said in a soothing tone.

"What, then? My parents?" Bronson had been feeling uneasy lately, but he'd attributed the vague, free-floating anxiety to the inevitable worry that accompanied rearing a teen.

"No, you were right the first time. It's Christopher—"

"Did he get into a fight? If so, I'm going to tan his hide so hard he'll think he spent a week in the tropics—"

"If you'd just let me get a word in..." Brandy gently admonished.

Bronson took a deep breath. "You're right. I'm sorry. I'll calm down."

Hearing Brandy's hesitation at the other end, Bronson felt his heart race and his palms sweat.

"You know I've had some of the boys work with the girls, to prepare them for the conference meets, and state."

Visions of Christopher overpowering some fragile junior girl crowded his vision, turning it red. With his serve, his son could really hurt someone.

As if reading his mind, Brandy said, "And no, he didn't mouth off, or nail someone on the court. I only let him hit with my top varsity player, Sabrina. And she can hold her own.''

Bronson had heard Christopher's wild ravings about the number one girl player at the beginning of the school year, when Christopher had confided in his father his hopes of being accepted into Notre Dame. That had been before the deluge for orders at the factory, when Bronson had been forced to put in twelve-hour days and seven-day weeks at work just to keep up with the demand. He'd been trying to come home earlier the past couple of weeks, but lately his son never seemed to be home.

Impatient to get to the bottom of this, Bronson looked at his watch. A client was due any moment.

''Okay, so he's not hurt, and he didn't harm anyone. So what's the big deal?''

''Did Christopher mention a girl named Hayward? Sabrina Hayward?''

''Yeah. He enthused about her when school started, but he hasn't said anything lately.''

The silence at the other end of the line grew ominous.

Clenching his teeth, Bronson asked with deceptive mildness, ''What does this Sabrina Hayward have to do with Christopher?''

''I'd noticed how friendly Christopher and Sabrina had become during practice, but I thought they were just friends. It's quite common for competitors at their level to seek other juniors who can identify with the pressure they are under.'' From Brandy's gentle tone, Bronson could tell that his cousin was warning him to keep cool. But she'd better not talk about pressure. Pressure was working your way through school, and not knowing if there would be enough money to eat, let alone graduate. ''They were supposed to hit together this morning with my assistant coach, since Christopher was being scouted at Notre Dame this afternoon and Sabrina has a tough invite coming up. Well, my assistant coach called in sick this morning. Imagine my surprise when I went over to the courts, and neither Christopher nor Sabrina was there."

Bronson's insides clenched into a rigid knot. "And?"

"I was worried, because they are both good students and responsible athletes."

Bronson could tell his cousin was trying to soften the blow that was coming. But all she did was heighten the suspense...and it was killing him.

"Out with it, Brandy! Why isn't my son in school?"

"I made some discreet inquiries, and finally found out that Christopher was certain he'd get a scholarship from Notre Dame, and he wanted Sabrina to be with him."

Brandy paused for a moment before delivering the final blow. "They've decided to elope."

Tamara Hayward finally located the object of *her* frantic search: a late-model, shiny black Mustang. How could Sabrina have been so inconsiderate?

After all the late-night talks they'd had, after all the times Sabrina had deplored the subservient attitude of many of the cheerleaders at her school—as well as some of the other young women—who chased the football players like groupies, neglecting their own studies and ambitions simply to be part of a group, to belong, to make sure they would have a warm body on that all-important teenage altar, the Saturday night date—how could Sabrina have pulled a stunt like this?

When Meghan Donahue had stopped by the house that morning, Tamara had been in a rush. She'd overslept, which was unusual in itself, because even though Tamara was not a morning creature, she practiced punctuality like a religion—and she had been surprised to open the door so early in the day to her daughter's best friend.

"Hi, Meghan. Did your car break down?"

Meghan had looked at the floor in the living room as if it contained the answer to life's riddles.

"No, Mrs. Hayward. Sabrina swore me to secrecy, and I hate to betray her like this...."

Tamara had looked down at the girl's curly red hair and felt the first stirrings of doubt.

"What is it, Meghan? I know you only have Brina's best interests at heart, and I'm sure she won't mind your telling me. Is she flunking something? Did she get called into the principal's office?"

Meghan's hazel eyes were positively tortured as she raised her head and looked at Tamara.

"Sabrina is going to hate me for this, and I know she will never count me as her friend again, but I just have to—"

Alarmed, Tamara grabbed the girl's shoulders. "Yes, Meghan. What is it? Is she sick? Did she get into a car accident?"

"She's eloping with Christopher Kensington, the boy she's been going with since school started, right after the Notre Dame recruiter checks Chris out."

Bronson saw the parking space in front of the Eck Tennis Pavilion and went for it. The spot was right next to Christopher's Celica—the vanity plates read ACE ME 1.

His quick instinctive maneuvering earned him a loud, enraged honk. Looking behind him, Bronson saw a blond woman raise a frustrated fist at him.

He shrugged his shoulders. He'd cut her off, and was not a damn bit sorry. He had more important things to worry about than hurting the sensibilities of a spoiled rich brat driving her daddy's brand-new Continental. The fact that he was driving a Porsche did not dawn on him. The only thing that concerned Bronson was finding that thoughtless son of his and teaching him the facts of life—and not the kind he was sure Christopher had been learning from that little hustler he'd met just weeks ago.

* * *

The nerve of the man! Tamara hit the steering wheel with her fist... and regretted it.

Gingerly rubbing her hand, she reflected that there were obviously no gentlemen left. That jerk had seen her aim fulminating looks—and a hand signal or two—in his direction, but had ignored her as if she'd been no more than a pesky fly circling his picnic table.

Well, she had more important things to worry about. And she needed to channel her hostility toward its true source. Sabrina was now a senior, albeit a modified one. Her daughter was so bright she had been able to complete her high school credits in three and a half years—and in a matter of weeks would be a high school graduate.

As she pulled into a no-parking zone, Tamara felt deep pangs of regret. Not only was she losing her baby, but her baby was losing far more. Besides her innocence, Sabrina was forsaking her chance for a promising future, a great education and possibly superstardom.

Young love was wild, impulsive, crazy.

But did it have to be *stupid?*

Bronson located Christopher right away. He was down in one of the courts, warming up with a talented youngster. The young boy, a slender blond who was either precocious or small for his age, had a forehand any pro would envy. He was giving Christopher a run for his money.

As the two played points on the farthest court, hitting winners from the baseline as well as the net, Bronson realized his son's opponent might well be beating him handily if only he had a stronger serve. That—and the slight speed advantage Christopher's long legs gave him—were the only things keeping him from being blown off the court.

* * *

Tamara looked at her daughter and her eyes grew moist.

Despite her anger, rage and disappointment, maternal pride overrode all other feelings. Sabrina was damn good—better than the boy she was playing. He had muscle, speed and a more developed all-court game on his side.

But Sabrina's tremendous raw talent and fearless competitive spirit was making the boy run all over the court.

As her daughter hit a cross-court forehand winner, followed in quick succession by a down-the-line backhand and a searing volley, Tamara could not keep from applauding.

A man turned, a heavy frown on a handsome face dominated by incredible blue-gray eyes. Tamara stared him down. She knew it was bad etiquette to cheer, to make any kind of noise when two competitors were on the court.

But this was just a practice match. And if the stranger was one of the coaches evaluating the young man's talent—a young man who she was in no doubt was the hated Christopher Kensington—well, then, Tamara was happy Sabrina was giving such a good account of herself.

A screaming return down the line brought forth that maternal pride once again, and Tamara found herself applauding—a bit more discreetly this time.

But the man did not take kindly to her partisanship, and he left the railing over which he'd been draped to come to her side.

"Have you ever read the *Rules of the Game?*"

His rude, superior tone incensed Tamara. He was the dark-haired boor from the parking lot. His arrogance extended not only to taking other people's parking spots—next time she'd make sure not to bother extracting a bothersome eyelash until a space was safely under her wheels—but also to instructing hapless onlookers.

Well, she could teach him a thing or two about the rules of the game—and not only in tennis.

"Oh, you mean as in the rules of parking? As in the unspoken rules of etiquette? Well, I guess according to you, take your eye off a parking spot for a millisecond, and *voilà* ... it's gone!"

The transformation in the man's expression would have been funny had Tamara not been so incensed. His next words did nothing to make the day any brighter.

"Oh, you're the girl—*woman*—from the parking lot. You're a lot older than I thought...."

Had Tamara not gone through an emotional wringer for the past few hours, her customary sense of humor might have come to the fore. But this cretin had picked the wrong day to antagonize and insult her.

"And charming to boot," she told him icily as she straightened to her full five feet six inches.

A dull red tinged the man's chiseled cheekbones.

"What I meant to say was, I thought you were a teenager, a college student—"

"Oh, and rudeness to young people is excusable?"

"No, what I meant was—" Flustered, Bronson tried to recover lost ground. "If you would do your makeup before you leave the house—"

"My makeup!" That tore it. Not only did Tamara not use makeup—to Sabrina's eternal dismay—but she would never sit in a car admiring her face in a mirror. Luckily, good genes had provided her with the youthful, blooming quality of a woman ten years younger than her thirty-nine.

"I bet you use your big frame to crowd your way to the front of the line at sport events, or buffets, or bathroom lines. If I'm not mistaken, you also go through the express checkout with thirty items, and pop out a checkbook or credit card."

His gaze narrowed. "Listen, if I wasn't busy watching this match—"

"Practice match," Tamara interrupted. "And apparently you weren't too damn busy to come over and complain." Tamara didn't care if she sounded rude. This man really did rub her the wrong way, and it wasn't only because he was as good-looking as her ex-husband. She had sworn off handsome men, and this Neanderthal would be on her blacklist . . . right at the top.

"You should talk," the man shot back. His eyes kept going back to the match, and he told her, "I'd love to spar with you some more—"

"Don't bother!"

"—but I've better things to do."

As he turned to leave, Tamara asked sweetly, "Oh, you mean you finally remembered you were scouting that rather mediocre young man?"

Six feet of muscled, lean flesh whipped around on a dime.

"I'm not watching the little guy. I'm watching the six-foot-two genius."

"You call that genius?" Tamara kept her voice low, because the two teenagers had not noticed their presence, so engrossed were they in their practice match. "He's just passable—good one-handed backhand, adequate slice and serve, good retriever. That's about it."

"Good retriever?" The man once again approached Tamara. "That boy has excellent speed, and a great backhand volley and groundie. His serve clocks in at almost one hundred and twenty an hour on flat ones—and he still has not finished growing!"

Since Sabrina was only five-two—although she'd been projected to grow to a respectable five-seven in the next year or two—height was a sore subject with Tamara.

"Being bigger and more powerful is the only thing your 'genius' has over his opponent, because he loses in the raw talent and creativity department."

"'Raw' is the right adjective," the man said condescendingly. "And when a player does not possess a complete game, he can afford to be fearless...after all, what pressure is there on an inferior player to beat a superior opponent?"

"Inferior? Are you so blind you can't spot true talent?"

"True talent? What's the matter with you? Are you—?" Suddenly a crafty look came over the man's face. His wide forehead smoothed out, and the two laugh lines bracketing his sensual mouth deepened. "I get it. You're an opposing scout, and are trying to psyche me out. Don't worry...I'm not in the game of recruiting. You can have Christopher."

Was there no end to the conceit of this man?

"Were I in the business of recruiting, you wouldn't stand a chance," Tamara threw at him. "Besides, I'd do a lot better than that overgrown *orangutan* down there—"

"You are really something," the man said with a smile that suddenly caused Tamara's hormones to zing. He turned his head to glance at the kids.

Tamara breathed a sigh of relief. "They're done."

She looked down on the courts from the open balcony. Ordinarily she would have been on the upstairs viewing area, but this goon had kept her from assuming her normal vantage point.

Now she looked on as both Christopher and Sabrina toweled off, coming together as if drawn by a magnet, their bodies almost touching. She wasn't sure how they could even dry off with so little space between them.

Her stomach knotted. She was sure Sabrina had given her an ulcer, something her high-powered career had not managed to accomplish.

So lost was Tamara in grim thoughts that she had missed part of what the odious man was saying. He'd grabbed her arm and propelled her forward.

Leaning over the balcony, his anger temporarily on hold, Bronson called out, "Christopher, come meet this woman coach. She's really—"

Bronson stopped in midsentence at the horrified look on the youngsters' faces.

Both teenagers dropped their towels, their expressions mirror images of shock.

"Dad!"

"Mom! What are you doing here?"

Two

The shock passed from children to parents.

Tamara and Bronson swung toward each other as if suspended by the same puppeteer.

"You're—"

"You've got to be kidding!"

Sabrina and Christopher exchanged puzzled, and relieved, glances. As long as attention was diverted from them, they welcomed the respite.

Bronson was shaking his head, as if dazed. "*That's* Sabrina Hayward?"

The condemnation in Bronson Kensington's tone elevated all of Tamara's motherly hackles.

"I told you she was good!"

"Yes, for a girl," Bronson said, his expression stormy. It was obvious he was undecided as to whom to tear into first: his wayward son, the troublesome girl who had led him astray, or the mother of the player who had been giving his son fits on the court.

After Meghan's revelation, Tamara had ample reason to distrust the Kensingtons. Bronson's less-than-diplomatic words did not smooth the waters.

"Sabrina is good. Period. It's obvious from your chauvinistic, superior attitude where Christopher got his bad judgment. I guess his irresponsible behavior toward my daughter is not entirely his fault, considering the example you set."

"My example!" Bronson exploded. He regarded Tamara Hayward with intense dislike. He had obviously underestimated the opposition. If Sabrina was anywhere near as whip-smart and determined as her mother, Christopher did not stand a chance. Alone, that is.

But then, Christopher would never have to face anything alone, not as long as there was a breath left in Bronson's body.

Belatedly noticing some college kids and alumni watching their heated debate with interest, Bronson said stiffly, "Do you think we could carry on this conversation somewhere more private?"

Tamara blushed, mortified. She had always considered herself a cool customer, and was seldom flustered under even the most adverse circumstances.

Her daughter's well-being and future, however, could not begin to compare to any financial transaction or career consideration. She'd just have to assume the same objectivity and astuteness when dealing with Bronson Kensington as she did with any business adversary. More important, it would behoove her to make Bronson an ally, rather than an enemy—or at least, a bigger enemy than he already was.

Trying for an even tone, Tamara said, "All right. Should we continue our discussion at a restaurant after these two young people get a chance to clean up?"

Though at first ready to debate her suggestion, Bronson Kensington seemed to reconsider his tactics. Both parents had a lot to gain by teaming up.

The teenagers were already presenting a united front.

Turning to his son, Bronson said authoritatively, "Christopher, we'll wait for you outside. Be there—pronto."

"Dad," Christopher said, his handsome, broad face acquiring a stubborn set, "I'm eighteen. You don't have any right to order me around."

"I'm paying for your training, car, living expenses—as long as you live under my roof, you will do as I say."

"That can be changed, Dad. I can always get a job during the day and study for a GED at night."

Sensing dangerous undercurrents, Tamara quickly intervened. "Perhaps we could all discuss this like adults, without any threats or ultimatums? Have you chil—aces had lunch yet?"

Sabrina spoke for the first time. "No, we haven't, Mother." Tamara winced at the sudden change of Mom to Mother. "But I also don't appreciate your having followed me here. I am *seventeen*, after all."

Tamara refrained from reminding her that Christopher could be accused of contributing to the delinquency of a minor and some other ugly charges. She did not want to issue any ultimatums, because she knew how strong-minded Sabrina was. Daughter took after mother in many ways, and strength of character was one of the characteristics they shared. Tamara shuddered to think that if she or Bronson pushed too hard, Christopher and Sabrina might not agree to talk to them at all, and might very well carry out their original plan.

A deathly chill went through Tamara. She wanted her daughter to be an independent, mature young adult.

She did not want to lose her only child simply because she and Bronson were not able to control their tempers—even if their anger and sense of betrayal were completely justified.

"I'm sorry you feel that way, Sabrina, but you know with everything that goes on nowadays, I worry about your safety constantly."

"You knew I was safe, Mother," Sabrina challenged, her posture defiant, her green eyes cool. "I was with Christopher."

At this, Bronson stirred, and his gaze locked with Tamara's. It was obvious that, in this, they were on the same wavelength. But still, *his* son did not stand to lose as much as *her* daughter. Boys, or men, never did. Women were in higher jeopardy in every department.

Resisting the urge to tell Sabrina that Christopher, at the moment, represented her main worry, Tamara merely said, "I would like to discuss some things with you, if you don't mind. I think you'll agree I'm entitled, after I drove almost three hours when I found out you skipped school today and didn't tell me where you were headed."

Tamara held her breath, awaiting her daughter's response. Sabrina had always had a strong sense of fair play, and Tamara hoped her appeal to her daughter's fairness would succeed where threats would not. When Sabrina said nastily, "Obviously, someone snitched, or you wouldn't be here," Tamara thought she had failed.

But then Sabrina's stance softened slightly, and she added, "Okay, Mother, we'll meet you. But at our South Bend motel room."

Pinning Christopher with a laser look, Bronson roared, *"Your motel room?"*

"You've always emphasized the value of a dollar, Dad," Christopher said, the mixture of defiance and defensiveness in his posture revealing his extreme youth. "And you have to admit, one room is cheaper than two."

Instinctively placing a hand on Bronson's arm, which felt like corded steel under her cold fingers, Tamara jumped in verbally before Bronson could jump his son physically. "Wouldn't it be better if we ate first?"

Noticing that Bronson's words had further unified and alienated the kids, she suggested two of Sabrina's favorite foods, trying to keep the trembling out of her voice. "How about getting some pizza, or maybe a steak with fries?"

"You know I don't eat that greasy food anymore, Mother. Besides clogging the arteries, it's bad for my quickness on court. We'll meet you at the Knight's Inn—or not at all."

Tamara looked at Bronson, and would have laughed if she had not felt so much like crying. Apparently not a man used to remaining quiet, he looked as if he were about to suffer from apoplexy. His strong features were red and strained, and his blue-gray eyes shot off silver sparks. But there was deep pain behind them, which he was trying very hard to keep from his son.

Tamara felt a huge lump in her throat, and had to blink back a burning moisture from her own eyes. She and Bronson had more in common than she'd thought at first. They would really have to get on the same page if they were to divert disaster.

"Is that okay with you, Mr. Kensington?" she asked softly.

Bronson looked at her with a distant expression, as if he'd forgotten where he was. Shaking his head, he told her, "Please call me Bronson. And no, it's *not* okay with me—"

Seeing Tamara's warning look, he smiled wearily at her, and added, "But I guess it'll have to do."

The children grinned at each other, acting as if they had won a major victory.

Tamara's throat closed again. How young and naive they were. They could win as many battles as they wanted, as long as she and Bronson won the war.

Putting his arm protectively around Sabrina's shoulder, Christopher told her gently, "Come on, Bree. I'll walk you to the locker room." Over his shoulder, he tossed at his father, "We'll see you two outside when Bree is done."

Not only did Bronson's large fists clench, but his whole body seemed to tense. Tamara feared again that father would attack son, and teach him a thing or two about manners.

Thankfully, Bronson was able to maintain control. She noticed the painfully visible way he forced his body to relax.

As the kids headed toward the locker rooms, Bronson muttered, "How touching."

Tamara swallowed, unable to speak. Turning to her and correctly interpreting her look of fear, Bronson gave a mirthless laugh. "Don't worry. I'm not about to kill my son. Yet."

Tamara nodded. "Good. My daughter would never forgive you." Carefully keeping her expression and tone neutral, she asked, "Do you think we could speak for a moment? Outside?"

"Going to beat me up? Go ahead. Take your best shot. You're right—I am at fault, if my son can act like such an ass."

"Let's refrain from violence and assigning blame just yet, shall we?" Tamara suggested, warming to Bronson Kensington despite herself. Although she wanted to be on his good side and seek his support for the matter at hand, she did not want to like him too much. All they had in common was the children—whom they were obviously both crazy about—and they needed a temporary alliance in order to separate them. Anything beyond putting aside their common distrust and uniting for the matter at hand was out of the question.

Although she resisted generalizing, in her own experience—which had culminated in her marriage to Robert—good-looking men were too attached to their own reflections. What made Bronson even more dangerous was that he seemed quite different from her ex-husband. And that was a problem: he was already causing curls of awareness in the pit of her stomach. How could she deal properly with this crisis if she behaved in the same adolescent manner as Brina?

Putting on the car coat she had taken off when she'd entered the tennis lobby, Tamara took a quick look at the framed pictures of the Notre Dame tennis teams, men's and women's.

"How can they think of throwing all this away?" Tamara murmured, unaware she'd spoken aloud.

"Maybe because they've both been so spoiled they don't know what life is really like," Bronson answered softly, his eyes taking in the smiling faces of the women's tennis team as they posed around the NCAA Championship sign.

About to protest, Tamara desisted. Maybe there was some truth in what he'd said. It would certainly be food for thought, when she had a free minute to dwell on it.

Right now they had to make sure they would be able to leave this campus with their respective children in tow.

And for that they would have to utilize all of their combined wiles and experience.

As they turned away from the pictures, Bronson touched Tamara's shoulder gently with his hand, and she found she liked its strength and assurance. Fighting against the pleasing sense of companionship his contact aroused, Tamara once again reminded herself of why she'd rushed over to Notre Dame.

And she reminded herself that Bronson was Christopher's father. Right now, he represented the enemy camp. If he happened to have more substance than Robert, well, she'd have to deal with it. He was fighting for his kid; she was fighting for hers.

His next words addressed her own sudden craving for some space and oxygen.

"Let's go outside, shall we? I really need some fresh air."

Three

"**I** don't believe it!"

Tamara looked at the spot where her car had been. Carjacking? In South Bend? On the venerable Notre Dame campus?

Tamara turned outraged eyes on Bronson and caught the smile he was trying to hide.

"What's so funny?" Tamara asked, even more furious. It was bad enough that Bronson had taken her parking space, but now he was laughing at her car's disappearance!

Speechless, Bronson pointed toward the street that bordered Alumni Field.

Her maroon Continental looked like a wounded animal, suspended from the rear of a tow truck as it labored down Ivy Road.

Burying her head in her hands, Tamara debated whether to laugh or cry.

To say this was not her day would be a vast understatement.

"Need a ride?" Bronson asked, lips twitching.

Tamara gazed at him through narrowed eyes. He looked quite handsome framed against the Eck Pavilion's geometric entrance. His hair, more brown than black in the pale sunshine, fell rakishly over his forehead, while his opalescent eyes regarded her with renewed interest.

Was he watching to see if she'd crack?

Squaring her shoulders, Tamara shored up her lagging spirits. Too much was at stake for her to come unglued over an inconvenience... even a major one like being left without transportation in Indiana, while she lived in Illinois.

"Thank you, but I think Sabrina can give me one."

Bronson kept staring at her thoughtfully, and then finally seemed to come to a conclusion.

"I owe you an apology."

"Oh?"

"You're not going to make this easy, are you?" Bronson asked with amused resignation.

"Any reason I should? I certainly have not had an easy time of anything today. Why should you?" But Tamara softened her words with a smile. She was curious to see what he had to say.

"First of all, I'd like to apologize for taking your parking space. I would normally say that anyone who parks in a no-parking zone deserves anything she gets for taking the chance, but under the circumstances..."

"You mean my being in the same desperate hurry that made you take *my* spot in the first place," Tamara supplied sweetly.

"Exactly." Bronson grinned. "I was consumed with worry, and I can see you were, too."

"And?"

"And I'd like to apologize for those cracks about your daughter. Up close, Sabrina looks nothing like a boy, but with that short hair, and stature—"

"Sabrina might be five-two, but she's due for a growth spurt soon. She just looks short next to that sequoia you call your son—" Tamara cut herself off when she realized Bronson had been teasing. "I'm sorry. I should not have called your son an orangutan."

"Apology accepted. Although I can see how you wouldn't be kindly disposed toward Christopher at the moment."

Tamara did not deny Bronson's statement. "I'm not too thrilled with either of the children right now."

"The *children* better not hear you call them that."

Automatically glancing at the entrance to the Eck Center to see if the kids were coming out, Tamara asked Bronson, "How did you find out about them?"

"A frantic call from my cousin, who's the head tennis coach at Deerbrook High."

"Brandy Cavanaugh is your cousin?" Tamara felt like adding that it was no wonder Christopher played number-one varsity singles, but knew the comment would be unfair. It wasn't nepotism that had gotten him the top spot: the boy really *was* talented. Although with the kind of build he possessed, he could have his pick of any sport.

Retraining her focus away from the inequities of gender-based athletic opportunities to the business at hand, Tamara asked Bronson, "How did Ms. Cavanaugh find out they were planning on eloping?"

"They were supposed to hit with Dale, the junior varsity coach, before first period. Christopher was to have been in school in the morning for a pre-Calc test, and then drive down here for his session with the scout."

Tamara nodded. "Sabrina mentioned something about hitting with the top dog on the boys' team before school because of the invitational coming up, which includes nationally ranked kids from out of state. She told me they were even coming from Kansas and Wisconsin. So when she left at five with an extra tennis bag, I thought nothing of it. She sometimes goes out with her friends on Fridays after classes or a home meet, and takes extra clothes with her."

"I guess they had it all planned. I certainly knew nothing about Sabrina. Did you know about my son?"

Tamara's smile was full of irony. "Did I look or sound like someone who knew what was going on? I know I've been putting in a lot of long hours at work, but I've always been able to trust Sabrina. She's never lied to me before— not about anything important—and I certainly never opposed her dating, as long as she kept her grades up."

"Apparently Brandy had heard some rumors about my son and your daughter, but she'd discounted them because of the envy factor. Being a top varsity player brings a certain amount of pressure and exposure, and jealous comments are always flying around. She told me this morning that she had confronted Christopher a few weeks ago, and he'd given her the old bromide about their being just good friends."

"And Sabrina mentioned your son only in passing, and only in reference to how good a tennis player he was."

"Brandy asked around and finally cornered my son's best friend, Jonathan, who finally admitted that our kids were really serious about each other, but since they anticipated opposition from us—"

"And they were right!" Tamara interjected, her whole being a twisted mixture of shock, betrayal and pain.

"—they thought it better to just shoot first, and ask questions later."

Tamara fought the traitorous tears that were threatening to roll down her cheeks. She strove for composure as Bronson's sonorous voice washed over her, calming the waves of hurt and anger which this morning's grim realities had stirred up in her.

"She checked to see if their cars were still there, and when they weren't, she called me. I left my foreman in charge, and

I really pushed the pedal. I was lucky the ever-present State
Patrol on I-90 didn't get me."

Tamara's gaze was grim. "Brina's best friend stopped by
early this morning. Even though Meghan and my daughter
live only a couple of blocks away from school, they both like
to drive there."

"Teenagers' love affair with cars," Bronson said, rotat-
ing his head and trying to rub some tension away from his
neck with a hand, which, to his surprise, was shaking.

Tamara smiled ruefully. "Despite their outspoken devotion to saving the environment, neither Brina nor Meghan
will hear of conserving energy or cleaning up the air through
carpooling." Looking at her own hands, she noticed she had
been wringing them so forcefully they were red and throbbing. Shaking her head, she said in a low, painful voice,
"Apparently, Meghan didn't sleep a wink last night, because of conscience pangs. She finally decided to tell me this
morning, and she bled with each word she uttered."

"The tribal code teenagers live by," Bronson said, shaking his head. "Thank God our respective teens' best friends
showed more maturity and responsibility than they did."

"Neither Brina nor Christopher is going to think so once
they find out who told on them." She shivered as the chilly
winds buffeting the campus exacerbated the icy feeling her
daughter's actions had engendered.

She was startled out of her tormented reflections when
Bronson's hands lifted the collar of her coat to protect her
against the rising wind. His fingers brushed against her
throat, and their warmth stayed with her long after he'd reluctantly lowered his arms.

"Why don't we sit in my car while we wait for the kids to
come out?"

Bronson's throaty tone was not lost on Tamara. She had
not misread the sparks that had flown between them, even
when they'd acted like two feuding roosters upon discover-
ing each other's identities.

Tamara looked at the silver Porsche. It would be crowded in that small two-seater. She was finding it harder and harder to view Bronson objectively, and sharing close quarters did not seem a good idea.

On the other hand, standing in the icy wind that promised rapidly dropping temperatures tonight was not very judicious, either. The last thing she needed was to come down with a cold or the flu. She was on overload right now, both physically and emotionally, and her immune system was probably too weak to fight any circulating virus.

Sighing, she nodded and followed Bronson to his car, feeling strangely like a lamb being led to the slaughter.

Bronson opened the door for her and then went around to the driver's side. Tamara ignored his long leg accidentally knocking into hers as he got in, and turned in her seat, ostensibly to look at him, but actually trying to put more space between them. Despite the two huge strikes against Bronson—his good looks reminding her of her ex-husband and his being Christopher's father—she felt the ripples of his sex appeal shrink the limited space in the car, steaming away the chill she'd felt outside.

Ignoring his all-too-knowing gaze, Tamara strove to remind them both of what was urgent. Even if their bodies seemed to have minds of their own.

"Meghan was almost hysterical. The poor kid was torn between loyalty to my daughter and concern over Brina's welfare. Meghan said Sabrina had told her Christopher and she were in love, and planned on getting married, no matter what. I guess they see each other as some sort of Romeo and Juliet. Of course, Sabrina knew exactly what I'd say. Marriage before she even tries to accomplish her goal of turning pro, or at least graduating from college, would be premature."

Bronson frowned. "Your daughter is thinking of turning pro? So is Christopher. We had discussed the possibility, but we weren't sure if he could pursue his dream unless he received a scholarship and got help from the USTA Touring Pro program. At his advanced level, I cannot afford to front the cost of a traveling coach for him, plus equipment and tournament travel all over the world.''

Tamara chose not to follow this trend in the conversation. It was bound to cause friction between them, and right now she and Bronson needed harmony and cooperation.

"I know what you mean. I've been so busy trying to make ends meet, attempting to pay for Sabrina's private lessons, equipment and tournaments—'' Tamara noticed Bronson's puzzled look. "If you're thinking of the Continental, it's paid up. It's the only thing I've kept from the errant eighties, when everyone thought the sky was the limit.''

"Your company went under?''

"They 'restructured.' '' Tamara could not keep the bitterness from her voice. "After getting my MBA in night school, and seven years of slowly but steadily rising through the ranks, Sports Science Comp showed me—as well as several other executives—the door.''

"No retirement benefits, pension . . . gold watch?'' Bronson asked sympathetically.

"Not even a pin,'' Tamara said. "I'm self-employed now, and run a consulting firm. But the hours and overhead are brutal, and I've tried to keep the ugly facts from Sabrina.''

"Which was undeniably a mistake,'' Bronson said quietly. Noticing that Tamara was still shivering, he reached into the back seat and grabbed a large green sweatshirt with NOTRE DAME emblazoned in gold on the front. "Why don't you put this on? I'm sure it'll fit over your coat.'' As Tamara held the sweater in her hands, he added ruefully, "I guess I was anticipating that Christopher would enroll here.''

"I guess you were,'' Tamara said, giving him back the sweatshirt.

She saw Bronson's look of surprise, and heard the uncertain note in his voice when he asked, "Would you like me to turn on the heat? You'll be even more chilled when you get into your daughter's cold car.''

Tamara felt like answering that he had turned on the heat already, but knew innuendo would not be appropriate at the moment. She had no doubt Bronson would retaliate in kind, and who knew what that could lead to?

And even though Bronson's kindness made her feel like a heel, she couldn't stray from her original mission here. She didn't dare to openly show her resentment of Christopher right now, because she needed Bronson. They needed each other. They had to solve one problem at a time: they had to stop their kids' foolish plans.

Looking about the luxurious interior, she said, ''You seem to be doing all right.''

''Appearances can be deceiving. I'm also self-employed, and find myself putting in a few more hours a day and still not coming close to the business I had in the mid and even late eighties.''

''I guess everyone is feeling the pinch in the nineties,'' Tamara agreed. Remembering his earlier comment, she said, ''You mentioned before that we'd been too easy on our kids. Do you think you spoiled Christopher that much?''

''My parents were not able to help me after putting my two older brothers through college,'' Bronson told her. ''I wanted Christopher to have everything he desired—he's never held down a job—and everything I never had... especially after the divorce.''

Starting up the car, Bronson turned on the heater. ''When it gets warm enough, you can take off your coat. Then you can put it back on when you get into Sabrina's car.''

''If that day ever comes,'' Tamara said wryly. ''Sabrina has always been a fast dresser—comes from all those years of being called on to play doubles after finishing her singles matches in ninety-plus weather. I'm sure that the delay is not attire-related.''

Bronson grinned. "I'm sure you're right." His gaze dropped to her mouth, and then lower still, taking in her curved but athletic form. When his eyes returned to her face, Tamara could feel twin flags burning in her cheeks. All of a sudden the interior of the car—as well as *her* interior—was suffocatingly hot.

Trying to distract Bronson from his disturbing scrutiny and her body from its traitorous response, Tamara said, "Your wife took you to the cleaners?"

"Cleaners?" Bronson asked, his face a blank, his voice husky. Clearing his throat, he recovered swiftly. "Ah, no. Joanna wasn't after my money. Just her freedom, and a 'meaningful career.' She hasn't seen Christopher in years."

Tamara shook her head. "Amazing, the parallels between our lives. Robert has not shown any interest in Brina, either."

A charged silence fell between them. Tamara felt as if she were swimming underwater, and knew that, without the specter of Sabrina's future floating in the intimate confines of the car, she and Bronson would have been doing more than talking.

Horrified at letting her body's demands arise at a time when her daughter's needs were paramount, Tamara fought the attraction. She forcibly removed her gaze from Bronson's frank, glittering one, and changed position so she could look out the passenger-side window.

Tamara could feel fear creeping into her in twisted tendrils. Was it possible that she had been so busy trying to provide Sabrina with material things that she had neglected her emotional sustenance? Tamara had never been one to doubt herself, but something was wrong if her only child had chosen to confide in someone other than her own mother.

Bronson's hand shot out and gripped both of Tamara's, which she'd been torturing in her lap. "Don't."

She looked up from their entwined fingers, startled. Even the slightest contact with him seemed to touch a chord deep within her.

"Don't blame yourself. We taught our children right from wrong. Life is not always neat, and it's not always fair. Don't let your daughter do a guilt trip on you, or she'll walk all over you."

Tamara wanted to protest that Sabrina was not that calculating, that manipulative. But today she had seen a side to her daughter that she had never known before—either because Sabrina had hidden it from her, or because her daughter had changed so drastically, so quickly, that Tamara had not been able to detect it.

And it was definitely a side that Tamara did not like. At all.

Bronson's other hand covered hers, squeezing them reassuringly. From the renewed tension in his body, Tamara could tell the children had come out of the tennis center.

Four

Nervously, Tamara opened the door and got out of the Porsche.

Sabrina looked at Tamara with condemning eyes. "Do you and Mr. Kensington know each other, Mother?"

Bronson had also gotten out of the car and had come to stand by her. Tamara could feel him stiffen next to her at Sabrina's insolent tone, and it took all of her willpower to keep from lashing out at this stranger, who was once her daughter, who stood so challengingly before her. Glancing pointedly at Sabrina's hand, which was held tightly in Christopher's, she said coolly, "Not as well as you know Christopher, Sabrina. Bronson and I just met today."

Since Sabrina had stopped addressing her as Mom today, Tamara had also dropped her own shortened version of Sabrina's name, Brina. It hurt like the very devil to do so, but if Sabrina wanted a war, she was going to get one. As Bronson had said, she could not show any weakness that either of the kids could capitalize on.

"Ready for lunch now?" Tamara asked.

"Christopher and I decided to eat later. We're not really hungry now, and it's better if he waits until the scout takes a look at him. He shouldn't play on a full stomach, because it'll slow his footwork."

"Well, I didn't have any lunch—or breakfast, for that matter. I'm sure your mother is in the same boat, since she has to work like the dickens to keep you in lessons and a private school. I vote we go out to lunch—there are plenty of restaurants in the nearby mall."

Christopher seemed ready to object to Bronson's peremptory suggestion, but after one look at his father's face he desisted. Perhaps he was choosing which battle to fight.

Tamara felt renewed stabs of fear. Sabrina was hot-tempered, very much like Bronson. She could be counted on to blurt out exactly what she felt. But if Christopher was the self-possessed type, who kept things close to the vest...well, she and had Bronson better stay on their toes.

"I'll ride with you, Sabrina. My car got towed."

"You parked it in a red zone, Mother?" Sabrina asked, her voice full of that unique blend of condemnation and superiority that teenagers seemed to master as soon as they hit those magical years.

Once again Bronson came to her rescue. Although it was unneeded, it felt good to have a man rise to her defense.

"Your mother was so concerned about you that she gave no thought to her job or her car. All she wanted was to make sure you were all right."

"How do you know so much about my mother?" Sabrina asked, her tone and expression vibrating with hostility.

"It'd be obvious to a blind person how much she cares about you. And as for the rest, the fact that she's single, yet manages to send you to a good school, pay for your car and tennis expenses means she must be sacrificing like mad on

your behalf. The least she deserves is some consideration,
and a hot meal."

An awkward silence ensued. It occurred to Tamara that
Bronson had hit the nail on the head. Sabrina was spoiled.
She had been given everything at great cost to Tamara, and
because her daughter had kept up her grades and worked so
hard at tennis, Tamara had tried to make everything else
easier for her.

She had ended up making it *too* easy.

"I'll follow you in my car, Christopher," Bronson told his
son.

After a slight hesitation, Christopher let go of Sabrina's
hand. "Will you be all right, Bree?"

Tamara could not contain herself. "What do you think I
plan on doing to her, Christopher? Beating her up? Kid-
napping her? Keeping her out of school like you did?"

"Christopher had nothing to do with my decision to skip
school, Mother," Sabrina said quickly, coming to the boy's
defense. "It was totally my idea to come here today and help
him warm up. The coach was delayed at a clinic he was giving, but he left word he'll still take a look at Christopher this
afternoon."

"Which means I won't be having any lunch, Dad," Christopher said pointedly. "You know I can't eat this close to
playing. And I don't want to keep the recruiter waiting. He's
going to be at the national tournament in Florida next
month, but he was interested enough in me that he said he'd
approve an early admission if he liked what he saw of me
indoors."

"Which means Christopher has to be back here in ninety
minutes, Mother."

Bronson and Tamara looked at each other. The teenagers' united front and fearless defiance signaled open war-
fare. This was going to be even harder than they'd
anticipated.

Without another word, Bronson and Tamara went their separate ways, Bronson to his car, waiting to follow Christopher's Celica, and Tamara joining her daughter in the Mustang.

Tamara buckled herself in on the passenger side of her daughter's car. It was truly humiliating to have had the Continental towed, today of all days, and after all the lectures she'd given Sabrina on being responsible for her car.

She would call the university from the restaurant and arrange to get her car later. Right now she wanted to have a little talk with her daughter, the stranger.

Bronson watched Tamara get into her daughter's car and admired anew the luscious curves and long legs that were elegantly folded into the Mustang. With her blond hair, gray eyes and youthful complexion, she looked more like Sabrina's sister than her mother.

Except when one got close enough to look into that steady gaze. He had read knowledge and experience there, which could only have been acquired through the bruising wringer of responsibility, bills, and single parenthood.

The pain visible in those luminous gray eyes was enough to make Bronson want to choke his own son—and her daughter. Instead of being grateful for all they'd been given, they had gone ahead with their own selfish agenda and had not even had the guts to confront either him or Tamara.

Bronson had just met the woman, and knew he had not made a great first impression. He planned on changing that. He understood what she was going through—hell, he felt as if he'd been branded with a hot iron that reached deep into his soul—and her only crime, like his, was loving so much she had put her kid's welfare and happiness before her own. Like him, she had sacrificed, tried to make up for a missing parent, and been betrayed by the person who had been the very center of her life.

Christopher and Sabrina might well be at the mercy of their hormones, and all the turbulence of adolescence in a world that made it increasingly harder to grow up. But they had been shown love, self-sacrifice, devotion. They were smart enough to know right from wrong, and nothing—not their raging hormones, nor the pressures from the outside world—excused their lack of honesty and, yes, downright betrayal.

"Why didn't you tell me about Christopher, Sabrina?" Tamara asked her daughter quietly as soon as they pulled out of the Eck Tennis Pavilion parking lot.

"I tried to, Mother," Sabrina said, smoothly maneuvering the car as she headed toward Angela Boulevard. "But you were always too busy."

"Oh, come on," Tamara said, shifting in her seat to look at Sabrina's expression. Her chest constricted. Her daughter might think she was an adult, but the baby roundness of her face, the innocent look in those green eyes...they spoke of a child protected against the harshest realities of the world, with its cruelties, unfair rules, and gaping jaw waiting to devour the unprepared.

Had she overprotected Sabrina?

Sabrina shot her a quick glance, and the hostility and coldness Tamara read there froze the blood in her veins.

"You know you were always too busy. The only things you cared about were that I got good grades and practiced hard."

Mystified, Tamara shook her head.

"And what is wrong with that, may I ask? You know you need good grades to get into a good university. And in order to have any chance at turning pro, you need a high national ranking—which would also allow you to get into top schools like Stanford, Northwestern, or Notre Dame—"

"What about my social life, Mother? Why should I have to give up everything?"

Anger shot through Tamara, and she had to contain herself to keep from raising her voice. "You know that the
reason you don't have a higher ranking is that I didn't send
you to more tennis camps, and gave you the choice to attend concerts and dances instead of participating in important tennis events—"

"It's all about tennis, isn't it, Mother?"

"What do you mean—all? You made a choice not to attend one of the tennis camps in Florida, or California. As a
matter of fact, I was quite willing to move to either coast so
you could play year-round and have more access to competition and world-class pros—"

"That's exactly what I mean, Mother!" Sabrina practically shouted. Shocked, Tamara looked at her daughter.
Only in the past few months had she even dared raise her
voice at Tamara.

"Sabrina, calm down. You're driving, remember?" Tamara reminded her as they approached an intersection. As
the light turned yellow, Sabrina slammed on the brakes and
swore.

Tamara paled and watched, speechless, as both Bronson
and Christopher, who had made the light, pulled over to the
side of the road to wait for them.

Another admirable trait of her daughter's was her self-
control. When her opponents were cursing up a blue streak
on court, she had always maintained a calm, reserved de-
meanor. A tournament director in Kentucky who had seen
Chris Evert play as a junior had compared Sabrina's
sportsmanlike behavior during matches to the legendary
champion's.

But this out-of-control teenager was nothing like the
daughter she had raised.

As the light turned green, Sabrina leaned on the acceler-
ator and took the turn with a squeal of tires.

"Sabrina, take it easy!" a horrified Tamara yelled as they
almost hit a car in the next lane.

Sabrina slowed down and swore again.

"Stupid jerk!"

"I'm sorry to say, Sabrina, but the jerk in this case is you. What's happened to you, anyway?"

As her daughter turned a wounded, confused look on her, Tamara regretted her outburst.

"That's what I mean, Mother. The only time you're ever with me, or have anything nice to say to me, is when I get A's or win a match—or preferably the damned tournament."

Expertly passing, Sabrina caught up to Christopher's Celica, which was the lead car, and motioned for him to open his window. When he did, Sabrina said, "Chris, let's skip the restaurant altogether. Let's just go over to the room and get this over with."

Christopher looked from Sabrina to Tamara, accusation plain in his gaze, and nodded. "You go ahead. I'll tell Dad, and I'll meet you there."

Bronson swore fluently, as he saw Sabrina head toward the highway. He was glad he was alone in the car, because he really felt like throttling the two kids.

Obviously, things had not gone too well with mother and daughter, since Sabrina had changed their plans and had indicated to Christopher that she did not even want to keep them company while they had some lunch.

Fear joined anger as Bronson followed his son to the motel. Had they lost before they had even begun?

Five

Tamara's throat constricted as Sabrina parked in front of Room 401. The door had a non-smoking symbol, and Tamara tried to swallow. At least Sabrina's rebellion had not extended to smoking.

Christopher and Bronson parked in adjacent spaces, and Christopher left the Celica as if shot by a cannon. Reaching the driver's side of Sabrina's car, he opened the door for her.

"Are you okay?" he asked Sabrina, his dark blue eyes drilling holes into Tamara.

Bronson left his car and opened the door for Tamara.

"Are you all right?" Bronson asked, *his* stern gaze drilling holes into Christopher.

If she hadn't been so exhausted from so many shocks in one day, Tamara would have laughed.

It was almost funny. Almost.

Mother and daughter answered simultaneously.

"I'm all right."

"I'm fine, thank you."

An awkward moment ensued as both Sabrina and Christopher searched for the hotel key.

Bronson and Tamara looked at each other, and Tamara saw the fear and disappointment she knew must be visible in her own eyes reflected in Bronson's gaze.

"I got it," Sabrina said, waving the brown plastic key chain.

Sabrina walked to the door, Christopher glued to her side. She opened the room and walked in, Christopher at her heels.

Tamara swallowed again and looked up at Bronson. Though his eyes were shadowed with worry, he gave her a crooked smile and put a supportive hand at her back as they walked into the Knight's Inn.

"Christopher has the best chance for a scholarship, Mom," Sabrina insisted. "And I want to be with him."

Tamara took a deep breath, and wrapped her hands around the knee of her crossed leg.

They'd been at this for the past twenty minutes. Both she and Bronson had been shocked beyond what they believed possible: both kids were putting their relationship above their futures and were refusing to listen to reason.

Tamara and Bronson were sitting on one double bed, facing Sabrina and Christopher, who occupied the other one.

While Tamara had been glad they'd not been confronted with a single, queen-size bed, she was not sure whether that was by design, or because they only had a room with double beds left when the children checked in.

At least, to her they were children. And to Bronson, too, she suspected. And they would be even when they got to be fifty, and had their own kids, and maybe grandchildren.

What was really eating at Tamara was that Bronson seemed distanced from her, now that he'd realized Christopher was still seriously considering attending college.

"Sabrina, you have one semester in which you can play a lot of tournaments and get your rankings up. And, if necessary, you can go to one university freshman year, and then transfer to one of the powerhouses in your sophomore year."

"Or turn pro then, right?"

"If you wish," Tamara conceded, frowning at Sabrina's disdainful tone.

"Haven't you heard a word I've said, Mother? I told you, I don't care about tennis right now. I want to be with Christopher."

"So apply to the same school," Tamara said. "If you don't get in, you can always try again next year."

"Next year is too late!" Sabrina yelled, leaping off the bed.

Tamara paled. "Are you—are you pregnant?" she got out, feeling as if all the oxygen had suddenly been vacuumed from the motel room.

"That's just like you, isn't it, Mother, jumping to conclusions."

"I think your mother has every right to ask that question," Bronson said quietly. "Otherwise, why would you be eloping?"

"We had planned on eloping because Sabrina and I want to be together. Haven't you two listened to anything we've had to say?"

"We've been listening, but nothing that either of you has been saying has made any sense," Tamara said.

Sabrina looked at Tamara with an expression bordering on hate. Tamara shivered and clasped her hands tightly together.

"Who told you where we were, Mother? Was it Meghan? I'll never speak to her again. If it wasn't for her, you wouldn't have found out."

"I thought you just told us that you had changed your minds about eloping," Bronson interjected.

"Yes, we did," Christopher said. "But that doesn't mean we're not planning on getting married soon. We'll wait until Sabrina graduates this January. She'll work during spring semester, while I finish high school, and I'll work too, during the summer. Then we'll both live on campus—Notre Dame has accommodations for married students."

Tamara jumped off the bed as Christopher was talking. She let him finish, and then went to stand in front of her daughter.

"Sabrina! What do you mean, you'll be working? What about all your plans for turning pro? And especially for an education?"

"Things change, Mother," Sabrina said, retreating from Tamara's wrath and snuggling closer to Christopher, as if for protection.

More than anything, that little gesture destroyed Tamara. She stumbled backward and felt for the bed, encountering instead Bronson's hand, which helped her sit down.

Normally Tamara would have been furious at seeing pity and sympathy in Bronson's eyes, but right now she felt totally numb. Sabrina had acted as if her own mother were a monster, someone she needed to be defended against.

Sabrina had until very recently looked up to her, and imitated her in many things. They'd been mother and daughter. They'd been close friends. For her whole life Tamara had put her daughter first, and now Sabrina had withdrawn from her. Totally.

Tamara felt like withdrawing herself. The pain was horrifying, worse than when she'd fallen from a tree and broken her leg and her wrist; worse than when she'd given birth to Sabrina in a natural labor that seemed to stretch into an infinity of endless agony.

As if from far away, Tamara heard Bronson talking. "—and you know how strongly I feel about your continuing your education, Christopher. But why should Sabrina have to give up hers?"

"Because if I plan on turning pro, Dad, someone has to help me type the term papers, do the homework, and practice. Sabrina can take a couple of lessons a week to stay sharp, so that I'll be able to hit with her. She's the best warm-up partner I've had yet."

The egotism of the statement would ordinarily have had Tamara attacking it and its issuer vigorously. But she was still reeling from Sabrina's uncharacteristic, cruel behavior.

It was again Bronson who stepped in. "I think Tamara had a point about wasting Sabrina's talent. And her education. Have you thought about her welfare?"

"Since when have you cared about anything other than my turning pro, and having everything you never had, Dad? Do you have the hots for Tamara?"

Bronson stood slowly, removing his hand from Tamara's, clasped tightly in her lap. He had seen red before when it came to his son—what parent of a teenager hadn't?—but this was too much.

"It's Ms. Hayward to you, boy. And you will apologize to her immediately."

Christopher tried to look defiant, but apparently the sight of his father's rigidly held body and the sound of his low growl reached him.

"Sorry, Ms. Hayward," he mumbled, drawing closer to Sabrina.

Tamara shook her head. If he was really sorry, he would think of Sabrina's future first. Of her well-being. His apology, forced as it was, didn't signify anything. And Christopher's was not the apology she wanted.

"Why, Brina?" she asked, unconsciously using the nickname. Her throat was arid, and she swallowed so that the words could come out more coherently. "Why do you want to throw your future away? If you don't want to turn pro, fine. If you don't want a tennis scholarship, that's fine by me, also. I'll try to come up with the money to pay for all four years of school. I'd hoped you'd attend Yale or Northwestern, but any school would do." Her hands extended in unconscious supplication. "Only don't just quit on everything—particularly yourself. You're too bright, too talented, to let these precious years pass you by."

"Are you any happier, Mom? You don't have a love in your life. Can you tell me that having a career has fulfilled you?"

"I can tell you that when your father and I divorced, it was hard at first. But you were always my priority. And a career has satisfied, me, yes. College and a career are not for everyone—men or women. But I know you, Sabrina. You will be sorry—maybe not now, or next month, or even next year, while you're living this fantasy. But you *will* be sorry— and then it will be too late to do anything about it—especially about your tennis. Don't let life pass you by."

"Life will pass me by if I can't be with Christopher. I'm choosing love over career, Mother."

Tamara let her hands fall to her sides. She could not take everything in at once. She would have to regroup, because she could not reconcile this hostile, changed young woman with the child that she had worshiped, adored, and put above all else.

"Being with Christopher doesn't mean you have to give up tennis, Sabrina," Bronson said, kneeling in front of her so as not to intimidate the girl. "You can still pursue your dreams, and especially your education."

"My only dream is to be with Christopher," Sabrina said stubbornly. She looked up at the boy, who returned her adoring look.

Tamara tried to throw off the lethargy of shock from her body. This was her baby, for heaven's sake!

"What made you change your mind about eloping, Sabrina?"

"I didn't want to go through all the hassle of you forbidding me to marry Christopher. I figured that someone would snitch. I didn't think it would be Meghan!"

"Yeah, Dad. Who told you? One of my 'friends'? Jonathan, maybe?"

"As a matter of fact, it was my cousin, Christopher," Bronson said.

"Brandy?" Christopher said, his tone horrified. "I thought she was cool, that she'd be on my side."

"That's why you went to her, and told her all about Sabrina, the girl you planned to marry, right?" Bronson said sarcastically. "Why did she have to find out through the grapevine? Or is it that you were afraid, and ashamed of acting like less than a man?"

Bronson's harsh words brought a crimson tide to his son's cheeks. "I *am* a man, Dad. I'm eighteen, and I plan to marry Sabrina."

"That's right, Mother," Sabrina said. "I turn eighteen in a few weeks, and we decided we'd wait until then."

"Why the single room, then?" Bronson said, looking from Sabrina to Christopher and letting his gaze linger on his son. "Anticipating the honeymoon?"

"Now you're sounding like a puritan, Dad. I didn't know you could be so square. And I told you. We got one room because it was cheaper than two."

Tamara took a deep breath. "Well, you were right, Sabrina. I do not approve of your throwing your life away. But what hurts the most is that you didn't even tell me how serious you were becoming about Christopher."

"You were always too busy with your precious career, Mother," Sabrina said defiantly. "And as obsessed as you are about my turning pro and graduating from the proper school, would you have been thrilled knowing that I had a boyfriend?''

''You've had boyfriends before, Sabrina,'' Tamara said tiredly. ''And you know you could have had a higher national ranking if I'd have pushed more for your tennis. But I wanted you to have a social life, and don't tell me now you didn't. While other kids were taking part in every major tournament, you attended dances, concerts, and sleepovers.''

''Well, none of that stuff means anything to me. The only thing I care about is Christopher.''

Tamara looked at Bronson. They seemed to be on the same wavelength, silently acknowledging that nothing else could be accomplished right now. It had been too much of a shock both for parents and teenagers today, and they had both taken turns being accusatory and on the defensive.

''You already missed the Friday meet today, Sabrina. What about your invitational tomorrow?'' Tamara asked as she rose from the bed. ''What about your responsibilty to your school, and to your teammates?''

''They'll survive without me, Mother. If it'll make you feel any better, help you save face, you can tell them I injured my ankle or something. I've been having tendonitis lately, anyway.''

Tamara looked from her daughter, dressed in a black warm-up suit, to Christopher, who was very handsome in dark green sweats. Sabrina appeared even tinier, more fragile, next to the muscular young man.

''This isn't about me, Sabrina. It's about your school, coach and friends. And it's totally your decision.'' Looking at Bronson, whose features were grim but breathtakingly masculine, she said, ''We'd better be going. I have to get Sabrina home, and Christopher has to get back to the tennis courts for his tryout.''

Six

"You go on ahead, Tamara. Christopher and I will take care of your car for you."

"Dad, I'm not going home without Sabrina," Christopher said, bristling.

The resemblance between the two was amazing, thought Tamara. Christopher was taller than his dad, and his shoulders were just as broad. He really would make a great quarterback, or tight end. And that of course would solve the problem of scholarships, which were so unfavorably tilted toward males.

Pushing back the habitual bitterness she felt over unfairness, and tragic loss and disuse of talent, Tamara brought herself to the present and forced herself to focus on the confrontation between father and son.

"I have to concentrate on my performance, Dad. I can't be worrying about Sabrina and a stranger's car."

Bronson stiffened, and his voice held equal steel. "The 'stranger,' as you so rudely put it, is the mother of the girl you profess to love. And if you didn't want to detract from your performance, you shouldn't have been monkeying around, and getting so serious at such a puppy age.''

"We're not monkeying around,'' Sabrina denied hotly.

"This is not puppy love,'' Christopher said, indignant.

Tamara and Bronson looked at each other. "If you're not sleeping together, then why did you get one hotel room?'' she asked quietly.

Sabrina actually blushed. "Mother, this is not any of your business.''

Tamara's laugh was strangled, incredulous.

"I wish you'd take us seriously, Dad. Remember, Sabrina will be eighteen in a few weeks.''

"But until then, she goes home with her mother. And had I known you were bringing a girl to a cheap motel—''

"It's not that cheap, Dad,'' Christopher objected. "That's why we rented only—''

"—one room?'' Bronson finished with deceptive softness. "And tell me, son, if you can't even afford a roof for one night over the head of the girl you love, how do you propose to pay rent, utilities, groceries—''

"We'll both work, remember?'' Sabrina said in an infuriatingly smug tone, moving closer to Christopher and putting her arm around his waist. "I'm graduating a semester early, and I can work until he graduates. We can also save the money he'll make giving tennis lessons at the club during the summer.''

"And then?'' Tamara asked, resisting the urge to shove her daughter away from Christopher and put her over her knee. She realized now why so many parents longed for the old days, when a good spanking was not considered torture.

"And then Christopher can go to college on scholarship, and I'll support us both until he turns pro.''

Tamara was bursting with the top-ten reality-check reasons, but she knew now was not the time. The kids were already on edge, Christopher had his meeting with the scout coming up, and they all had a long drive ahead of them. And they all could really use a good night's sleep. Sabrina might decide to go to the invitational in the morning, and Tamara herself had a lot of work to catch up on in the office.

Wearily getting to her feet—it felt as if it had been the longest day in her life—Tamara said, "Come on, Sabrina, let's go."

Sabrina put both her arms about Christopher's lean hips and stared at her mother mutinously. "I'm not going. You can't make me."

Tamara could almost have laughed at the petulant tilt to her daughter's beautiful lips. Almost.

"Sabrina, don't push me."

"Christopher, let go of Sabrina."

Christopher reluctantly moved aside, and Sabrina shot a murderous look in Tamara's direction. "You can't keep us apart, Mother. Not only will I run away the first chance I get, but I'll hate you forever."

Tamara looked at her daughter, so closely allied to a young man who was still wet behind the ears and a total stranger...allied against *her*. She felt as if her heart would be forever bruised.

Willing herself not to lash out, not to lecture, not to do anything but keep things relatively calm until she and Sabrina had a chance to hash things out in private, Tamara said, "Let's go, Sabrina. You have to be at Deerbrook at 6:00 a.m. for the Saturday invitational."

"I'm not going," Sabrina said. "And if you make me go, I won't play. I'll just fake an injury."

Out of the corner of her eye, Tamara saw Bronson breathe in deeply. That seemed like a good idea, because Tamara felt a double loss: Sabrina's throwing her future away at the same time she was managing to throw obstacles in the path of a possible relationship with Bronson. If only she and Bronson had not been unwittingly thrust into opposing camps!

"What happened to the code of honor you've always lived by, Sabrina? No cheating, no alibis, no excuses—always give it your best, and be as gracious in defeat as in victory?"

"That was for when tennis meant something to me, Mother," Sabrina said disdainfully. "Now the only thing that matters is Christopher."

Picking up her coat from the bed, Tamara got her purse and walked to the door. "Get your things, and let's go home, Sabrina."

Tamara opened the door and stepped outside, lifting her face to the welcome cool of the night. She gave one last look at Bronson as she closed the door behind her.

Winter was not far off. Autumn had always been her favorite season, but it seemed as if this year, fall would be a short affair.

Like Sabrina's dreams. And Tamara's own place in her daughter's life. Sabrina was willing to abandon everything for a boy, everything that had made her into a vital, happy, multidimensional person.

Tamara hated to think of what the death of a dream would bring.

At any other time, Sabrina's geisha shuffling of feet next to her as they went toward the Mustang would have amused Tamara. But now, it only brought poignancy to the ignorance, pain, intensity, splendor, and ultimately, danger of young love. First love.

"Do you want to drive, Mother?" Sabrina asked, sulking.

"As long as you promise not to kill us both, you can drive," Tamara said, getting in and stretching out her exhausted body.

"You know I would never kill you, Mother. Nor attempt to commit suicide." Meeting her daughter's indignant gaze as she turned on the ignition and automatically flicked on the lights, Tamara bit back the comment that came to her lips.

Sabrina was already killing her. Slowly.

"I don't see why we have to go through so much trouble for Mrs. Hayward. It's her car, after all, and if she was stupid enough to get towed—"

"Christopher!" Bronson's tone would have stopped a truck. "The reason Mrs. Hayward had her car towed was because I stole her parking space—"

"Way to go, Dad!"

"And the reason we're taking care of it is because you're the cause of her being here in the first place."

"Sabrina is *her* daughter," Christopher said defensively.

"Glad you remembered that small, insignificant fact. How would you feel if your own daughter cut school, and you didn't know where she was, and then found her with some punk—"

"I'm not a punk—" Christopher picked on the one element of his father's condemning statement that he could somehow refute.

"One, any boy that takes a girl to a motel room far away from home is a punk. And two, she doesn't know you from Adam. You could be a rapist, or a drug addict or a dealer."

"But I'm not—"

"Enough, Christopher. I'm tired, and I've had a hell of a day. Tomorrow I'll come back to pick up my car. Now let's get home. And don't you dare go even two miles over the speed limit, or your driving privileges will be revoked until further notice."

Christopher got into the Celica, and Bronson slipped behind the wheel of Tamara's car. At Bronson's signal, Christopher set off toward the Indiana Toll Road at a sedate pace.

Keeping an eagle eye on Christopher's car, Bronson realized he was disgusted with his son for yet another reason:

he'd just met an attractive, fascinating woman, and instead of having her next to him, Bronson found himself separated from her by more than distance.

Tamara opened the door to the town house, and the waves of hostility emanating from Sabrina followed her into the living room.

Normally, she would have started a roaring fire in the stone fireplace and ordered a pizza while Sabrina went to the local video store to rent a tape.

One look at Sabrina's set expression dissuaded Tamara from that idea. Instead, she asked quietly, "Are you hungry? I can fix you some—"

"Can't you get it through your head, Mother? I don't want anything from you. I'm old enough to do for myself, and I just wish you'd stop trying to control me."

Tamara took a deep breath. Obviously, some serious issues were involved here, and it was best if they were tackled with a rested, calm mind.

"Fine. There's a casserole and some cold cuts in the refrigerator if you feel hungry later. I'm going to make myself a salad, and you're welcome to share it."

Tamara knew Sabrina loved her "everything-in-it salad," which included the staples like lettuce and tomato, but also ham, blue and cheddar cheese and on occasion, shrimp.

This time, though, the ploy didn't work. "I'll just have a yogurt. I'm afraid I've lost my appetite."

You can say that again, thought Tamara. But she needed her energy, and she was damned if she was going to let Sabrina's moods dictate *her* eating habits—or anything else.

"Suit yourself," Tamara said, feigning unconcern.

She noticed Sabrina's surprise. Grimly, Tamara realized that her daughter was used to being waited on hand and foot, and having almost every whim attended to. Ordinarily, she would have been after Sabrina to eat something, but things were going to change around here, starting now.

Sabrina stalked over to the refrigerator, grabbed a strawberry yogurt and plucked a spoon out of the utensil stand—a wobbly, wooden contraption Tamara kept in the kitchen because Sabrina had made it for her in junior high. After ripping the plastic cover off the yogurt and stomping on the lever of the garbage can, she slammed the lid over the overflowing contents.

"You forgot to take the garbage out, Sabrina," Tamara reminded her, not liking her daughter's offended and offensive act one bit. If anyone had a right to feel offended and disappointed and angry, it was the mother kept in the dark—not the daughter acting like the Terminator with helpless appliances.

"If you had a husband, Mother, you'd have someone to do all these boring little chores."

Tamara went absolutely still. Holding her daughter's green gaze with her own darkened gray one, she asked, "Is that what this is about, Sabrina? Single parenthood? My failings as a mother? Are you blaming me for the divorce, and using Christopher as a replacement for your father?"

Sabrina lowered her eyes. She stirred the yogurt furiously, blending the fruit in the bottom until the creamy concoction threatened to bubble over.

Without answering, she flounced toward the kitchen door, but halted before leaving the room.

"What—what excuse are you going to give the coach about tomorrow?"

"Excuse?" Tamara felt sadness overwhelm her. All along she'd been hoping that if she kept her patience, Sabrina would come to her senses and make the responsible choice.

But apparently, another disappointment was in store.

"I'm not making any excuses, Sabrina. You either go, or don't go—it's your choice."

"You're just bluffing, aren't you?" Sabrina said, turning around and fixing her with a superior look. "Tennis has always been more important to you than to me. It's given you a purpose in life.''

Tamara laughed, and it was a rusty, pained sound that seemed to tear her insides apart.

''My purpose in life has always been your well-being and happiness, and my career. In that order. Tennis was important to me because it was a dream that would have allowed you to achieve much—primarily, utilizing your abilities to the fullest.'' Realizing she was being drawn into a lecture, something she'd promised herself she wouldn't indulge in tonight—and noticing the ''oh, no, not another lecture'' expression on Sabrina's face, Tamara said, ''From now on, Sabrina, you choose your schedule. If you want to attend practice early or late, participate in tournaments and meets, make an excuse or not . . . as you said, you're almost eighteen. It's all up to you.''

Turning her back on Sabrina, trying to keep sobs from ripping out her throat, Tamara went to the refrigerator and began gathering the ingredients for her salad with trembling fingers.

She sensed the moment Sabrina left the kitchen an instant before the door slammed behind her. Going to the sink, Tamara splashed some cold water on her face.

The shrill ringing of the telephone made her jump. Since Tamara had stopped by the office on the way home to pick up some work to catch up on over the weekend, she figured it had to be Christopher calling Sabrina. Sabrina had fumed over the time they'd spent in her office, but Tamara had calmly listened to all the messages on her answering machine, jotting down the most important ones, and had copied some disks she would need to use at home.

Now she dried her hands on a kitchen towel Sabrina had embroidered with the words The World's Best Mom what seemed like eons ago. Tamara almost dropped it when her daughter yelled, ''Mom, it's Mr. Kensington.''

Seven

"I hope I'm not disturbing you."

Tamara fought down the excitement that gripped her at hearing Bronson's baritone on the other end.

Now who was acting like an adolescent?

"No, of course not. We got home just a short while ago ourselves."

"Did you have trouble on the toll road or skyway?"

Tamara was warmed by Bronson's quick concern.

"No, no. Nothing like that. I just stopped by the office to get my messages and copy some disks. I'm snowed under, and I'm going to have to spend the weekend trying to catch up."

"The whole weekend?" Bronson asked.

Tamara's pulse sped up. "Why? What did you have in mind?"

"As you know, Christopher was not too happy about being separated—even temporarily—from Sabrina. He didn't play his best tennis for the recruiter, and he was a real pain in the butt when we went to retrieve your car."

"Oh, I'm sorry. I should have gotten the car myself—"

"That was my responsibility...I took your spot. And that was just his excuse to bellyache. He was really annoyed because he feels that at eighteen, he owns the world and has the wisdom of the ages."

"Same here. Sabrina has been carrying on like a martyr—a very offensive martyr—and was jumping out of her skin because she had to waste all that time at my office. She kept bringing up all the homework and tests she has to catch up on."

Bronson chuckled. "Highly logical. Here they are making plans to elope, and then they blame us for taking away a few hours of their very precious time." Tamara heard some noise in the background, and then silence. She figured Bronson had put his hand over the receiver. After a few seconds, Bronson came on the line. "Sorry about that. I've just taken away my son's driving privileges, and he cut a path of destruction on the way to his room."

Tamara sighed. "I'm afraid things are not much better with Sabrina. I'm so torn between telling her what to do and letting her take her lumps. I don't want to live my life for her, or through her. And yet I want to protect her so much, especially from decisions that I know will turn out to be awful mistakes."

"I know. We want to suffer every pain for them, take on all their disappointments and consequences. But they have to learn for themselves."

"I guess so," Tamara said glumly. Why couldn't personal choices be made with the same logic and planning as business decisions?

"As to the reason I called, I thought we should get together. I'll be picking up my car tomorrow, and I was wondering if you would care to accompany me to a banquet tomorrow."

"A banquet?"

"My company, Kensington Tools, has been nominated for an award for best working conditions and fastest growth in a small-business category. I know it's short notice—"

"No, no. I'd love to go."

Both Bronson and Tamara were surprised at her easy acquiescence. But Tamara was tired of responsibility, of worries and work and bills. Sabrina was ready to desert her, and Tamara was not going to put her life on hold anymore.

"Great!" Bronson said. "It'll be a formal affair, so I'll be wearing a tuxedo."

"Thanks for telling me. I guess I'll have to go out and buy myself a new dress."

"Please let me get it for you."

"No, thank you. I haven't had much occasion to dress up lately—except for success, whatever that means—and I'd love to go shopping for something that has nothing to do with work."

"I'll pick you up at seven, then."

"See you tomorrow."

Tamara put down the phone and realized that she felt like eating now. Bronson's call had cheered her up. Her appetite was not going to be the same for quite a while, until this nasty situation was resolved, but at least she would spend a few hours away from home tomorrow, in the company of a handsome man. She was surprised that Bronson had thought to ask her. Surprised and pleased.

About to go back to her salad, Tamara remembered Meghan. The poor girl was bound to be sick with worry. She truly was a good friend.

Tamara looked at the clock in the shape of a rooster, last year's Mother's Day present from Sabrina, and saw it was almost eleven. Still, she couldn't let Meghan go on worrying.

Picking up the phone, Tamara heard Christopher's deep voice, so similar to Bronson's.

"I tell you, my father has gone off the deep end. He just invited your mother to a banquet."

"A banquet! My mother? What did she say?"

"She agreed. I can't believe it! They're so old, they should know better."

"How could my mother betray me like this!" wailed Sabrina. "Here she goes ballistic over my going over to Notre Dame with you, and now she's dating your father? I mean, I want her to have a life—but your father? How could she—"

Tamara had had enough. She had never listened in on Sabrina's conversations before, but she figured turnabout was fair play. Had Sabrina not run away and put her through the wringer today, she could have laughed over the teenagers' opinions of Bronson and her "dating." Kids always thought of adults—especially their own parents—as somehow sexless.

But they had no right to listen in on conversations, or pass judgments on what fully responsible adults did— particularly since these two adults had been brought together by their own kids' planned elopement.

"Thank you for your concern, Christopher, Sabrina." She could hear Sabrina's gasp, and Christopher's sudden cough. "But what your father, Christopher, and what I, Sabrina, decide to do, is *our* business. I would appreciate two things. One, don't ever eavesdrop on us again, and two, please get off the phone, since it's late. And you, young lady, have a lot to do around the house tomorrow, starting with taking out the garbage."

Sabrina started mumbling some deprecatory remarks, but Tamara was having none of it. "Now, Sabrina, or your phone privileges will be revoked."

The two teenagers hung up with such force that Tamara was surprised the line was still working. She quickly dialed the Donahue residence.

* * *

Saturday came and went in a flash. Sabrina performed her chores with all the regal disdain of an oppressed princess. Tamara realized anew how much she had spoiled her daughter, not demanding much from her beyond getting good grades and doing well in her tennis. Tamara had wanted Sabrina to have a social life, not to miss out on the best years of her life.

Perhaps that had been a mistake in judgment. Perhaps she'd loved too much.

Luckily, she had so much work to catch up on that it was early afternoon before she surfaced, and she was mostly able to ignore Sabrina's loud sighs and door and drawer slamming.

Tamara came up for air when her stomach's grumbling reminded her that she had not had anything to eat since that grapefruit in the morning. Shocked, she realized that it was almost three, and she still had to shop for that special dress. The mall closed at five today, so she didn't have much time.

"Sabrina!"

"Yes, Mother?"

Tamara's lips twitched. Sabrina had covered her head with a scarf, and sported one of her aprons, which reached past her knees. She was playing the role of Cinderella put to work by the evil stepmother to the hilt.

"I have to go get a new dress. Want to come with me to the shopping center? You said you needed a new purse and boots."

"Go shopping with you? Are you nuts? I can't let my friends see me in the mall with you."

Tamara winced at her faux pas. Of course, she'd broken a cardinal rule. Whereas just a few short years ago, they had been almost inseparable, now mother and daughter seemed to be on opposite sides of the fence. Sabrina belonged to a teenage tribe that allowed no admittance to anyone older.

Refusing to let the hollow in her heart spread to the rest of her, Tamara resolutely concentrated on the task ahead of her: selecting an evening gown.

"Do you need anything from the mall, then?" Tamara asked as she went to get her purse and a windbreaker.

"How about a maid?"

That stopped Tamara midway to the door. Looking straight at her daughter, she said, "Why, Sabrina? Haven't we had one all these years? Namely, me."

Sabrina could not hold her mother's gaze. Zipping up her jacket in a vicious movement, Tamara left the house before she said something she'd really regret.

At precisely seven o'clock, the bell rang.

"I'll get it," Sabrina yelled from the living room, where she'd parked herself for the past few hours, watching two of her favorite movies, *Pretty in Pink* and *Aliens*.

Tamara came out of her study, where she'd been doing some last-minute work on a deadline while she waited for her date. She was glad she had purchased the desktop publishing program, because it allowed her to keep on top of her work both at home and in the office.

Hearing Bronson's deep voice, Tamara quickly downloaded and turned off her computer.

"I thought Christopher was driving you here," Sabrina said.

"Whatever gave you that idea?" Bronson was asking.

"Because you had to bring back my mother's car—she took mine to go shopping for her stupid dress today," Sabrina said accusingly, as if it were all Bronson's fault.

"And I brought the Continental back. Your mother can drop me off at home when the function's finished."

"I knew my mother was liberated, but doesn't this make you a gigolo?"

"Sabrina!"

Bronson's silver blue gaze went unerringly to Tamara's, and she stopped breathing.

He looked gorgeous.

And that was an understatement.

Certain men had been born to wear tuxes, and Bronson seemed to be one of them. With his broad shoulders, tapered hips, and shining dark hair, he was breathtaking.

She was absolutely stunning.

The white, Grecian-style dress she was wearing, off-the-shoulder with gold braiding at its waist and long hem, accentuated her lush curves and brought out the strawberry accents in her blond hair.

Their gazes locked, and he found breathing difficult.

Bronson almost forgot what he was going to say, but brought himself down to earth with great effort.

"What does it make Christopher if you work while he goes to school? A kept man?"

Sabrina frowned. She was whip-quick, and it was not often that she was stumped.

"But that's different."

"How so?" Once again, Bronson ventured a look at Tamara, but felt his heart do a bongo beat and quickly glanced down at Sabrina.

"Because he and I love each other."

"Well, who knows where my relationship with your mother will lead? We have you two to thank for bringing us together."

Distaste was obvious on Sabrina's full lips. "But you two are old, and besides, you're our parents... and it's like incest."

"So?" Bronson repeated. "Just break it off with Christopher, and there won't be any problem."

"That's exactly what you two want, isn't it?" Sabrina accused, bristling. "That's why you're going through the motions."

"Young lady," Bronson said, his tone forbidding.
"Nothing I might ever do with your mother could be re-
motely called 'going through the motions.' And you'd better realize that the world does not revolve around you—or
my son. Your mother and I have lives—apart from breathing and bleeding for the two of you."

"I don't begrudge my mother going out," Sabrina said,
squaring her slight shoulders. "I've often told her to get a
life."

"Well, now that she has, you presume to tell her with
whom to get it. Isn't that just what you're accusing us of
doing to you and my son?"

Sabrina opened her mouth, but Tamara forestalled her.

"Sabrina, we're running late. Why don't you ask Meghan
to come over and keep you company?"

"Because she's not my friend anymore. She snitched, and
I'll never forgive her."

Not about to let her evening be ruined by her daughter's
obstinacy, Tamara picked up her wrap and the small white-
pearl clutch from the back of the sofa.

"I should be back by two, Sabrina."

Bronson picked up her cape, and put it around Tamara's
shoulders.

"Two o'clock?" Sabrina's tone was horrified.

"You're right," Bronson said. "It might be closer to
three. Make sure you lock all the doors and windows."

Bronson's pronouncement left Sabrina speechless.

That was something quite rare, and just as precious, Tamara reflected. Exchanging an amused glance with Bronson, she dropped a kiss on Sabrina's cheek, who was too
shocked to move away, as she usually did when Tamara tried
to display any affection.

"You look exquisite," Bronson told Tamara softly, but
not low enough that Sabrina could not overhear.

As Bronson opened the front door for her, Tamara stole a last glance at her daughter. Sabrina looked positively furious, her light brows drawn together in a forbidding frown, her large eyes spitting green fire.

Eight

The banquet hall in which the dinner and awards presentation were to take place was one of three—the largest and most luxurious—in a German restaurant that had recently been renovated. It was located in Lincoln Park, a beacon of upward mobility. The surrounding neighborhoods were undergoing gentrification and the contrast between the oasis of elegance of Rheinische Nächte and some of the more prosaic establishments was that readily found in any large city.

The entrance to the restaurant was breathtaking, with a large chandelier imported from Vienna setting the tone. Tamara was reminded of the castles she had visited as a college student while touring Europe one unforgettable summer, and she was glad Bronson had invited her. She had forgotten how much she loved to travel and how she had become a virtual prisoner to her job.

She told Bronson so as they took their places at an exquisitely set table.

"I'm glad," he said softly, taking one of her hands in his own. "I've started to become housebound myself, and life has a funny habit of slipping by if one's not watching."

As their waiter approached to ask if they would like anything to drink besides the wines already at their table, Tamara took the opportunity to gently extricate her hand.

Things were moving too fast, and she was becoming far too attracted to Bronson. They still needed to settle the problem regarding the kids, and she had to be constantly on guard not to succumb to Bronson's powerful magnetism and charm.

As Tamara looked about the hall, seeing the crystal in the smaller chandelier and the dinnerware glow with polished elegance, she could feel Bronson's eyes on her. His gaze was almost palpable, and she found her lungs suddenly constricted, impeding normal air passage.

Nothing about this situation was normal.

Knowing she had to meet Bronson's gaze sooner or later, she steeled herself. His eyes held gentle knowledge, and his smile was rueful.

"You're not sure if this was a good idea after all," he told her, his smooth baritone washing over her skin like a feather, both delicate and unsettling.

Meeting both his gaze and her own feelings head-on, she nodded. "This doesn't feel right."

"Because you feel we are betraying our kids?"

"In a way. We are telling them they cannot feel a certain way—"

"—and here we are, experiencing the same emotions?"

"Well, I wouldn't say the *same*," Tamara told him, smiling. "I still think theirs is a puppy love, and there *is* the question of their futures being at stake. Sabrina is showing her immaturity by her displays of histrionics. Her eye-rolling, sighing and general, all-purpose slamming around the house is supposed to remind me how unfair I'm being, grounding her and requiring her to do housework."

"And you think we're being disloyal because we're having fun while the two poor dears languish at home."

Tamara laughed. She had been feeling guilty, but when Bronson put it that way...

"You're right. They did the wrong thing, cutting school, taking off without telling us, going to a motel...."

"And they deserve to face the consequences." Bronson paused as the waiter put baskets of freshly baked bread and rolls on the table. Once the white-jacketed waiter had left, he said, "Brandy tells me Sabrina never made it to the Saturday invitational, and they missed her. State is coming up soon, and without Sabrina's help, they might not make it this year. Brandy wasn't sure whether to be concerned about the excuse Sabrina gave regarding her wrist."

Tamara took a sip from her wineglass before answering Bronson.

"Sabrina has been having problems with her wrist ever since her private coach began changing her backhand from a two-handed to a one-handed stroke. But as you and I both know, that's not the real reason she missed the Friday meet and today's invitational."

"What do you say we enjoy the rest of dinner and get in some dancing without mentioning our kids for a while?"

Tamara smiled in agreement. "I think that's a wonderful idea."

The evening passed in a blur. The food was excellent, with choices from both German and American cuisine. The entertainment was eclectic, with German staples like waltzes and polkas, slow dancing, and faster tunes for the more adventurous.

The awards presentation proceeded at a rapid pace, with the winners making quick, graceful acknowledgments. Tamara reflected that the Oscars should take a cue from the way this affair was being run.

By midnight, though, Tamara was not able to contain or hide her anxiety.

"You're worried about Sabrina," Bronson said as he escorted her to the table after some dreamy dancing to "Tales from the Vienna Woods."

"I know she's almost eighteen, but she's never been alone in the house before. The few times I went out on a date or had a business affair that lasted late into the evening, she either stayed at someone's house or had a friend or two for a sleepover."

"She still hasn't forgiven Meghan?"

Tamara shook her head, and a tendril came loose from her soft chignon. Bronson tenderly took the blond, wispy hair, caressed it between thumb and forefinger, and curled it behind her ear.

"Would you like to leave?"

"I hate to cut the evening short—"

"If you hadn't come, I probably would have left already," Bronson told her, getting up from the table. They said goodbye to their tablemates and made their way out of the ballroom.

After getting Tamara's cape, Bronson suggested, "Why don't you call Sabrina to see if she's all right? We're so close to downtown, it would be a shame to waste the evening. We could at least savor the city from Lake Shore Drive."

Tamara had always loved the Chicago skyline, so she agreed.

Sabrina answered on the third ring.

"Are you all right, Sabrina?"

"Of course, Mother. I'm not a baby that you have to check up on. I can take care of myself. You know I'm almost—"

"Eighteen. I know." Tamara sighed. "But you know I worry about your safety, especially since you're in the house alone."

"If I had an apartment on my own, Mother, I'd also be alone. What would you do then? Call me every minute?"

Tamara couldn't argue with that logic, but that would be her very instinct. Yet how could she explain her natural worry to her teenage, invincible offspring? It was hard to let go of a daughter, to realize she was not a child anymore.

The only time Sabrina would understand Tamara's churning emotions and sense of profound loss was when she had her own daughter, and her child metamorphosed from a little girl in ponytails into a young woman with her own mind, own needs, and own life, which no longer included her mother as the center of it.

Blinking away tears, Tamara said, "Just checking. See you later."

Bronson's arm curved about her shoulder, and Tamara leaned into his solid warmth.

"Sorry," she said, hastily wiping her eyes. "I didn't mean to ruin your evening by turning maudlin."

"You didn't," Bronson said huskily. He bent and pressed a soft kiss on her cheek, licking a tear away.

Tamara's breath lodged in her throat. The gesture was sweet, tender, and incredibly sexy. She moved away from Bronson, raised her gaze, and was lost in the pool of emotions whirling in his dark blue eyes.

Bronson brushed his lips against hers, and the comfort he offered touched her very soul.

"It's hard, isn't it," he told her softly as his fingers caressed her wet eyelashes. "Letting go is hell."

"You too?" she asked, marveling at the closeness she felt toward a man she had started out disliking so intensely.

"Just because I'm a man and just because I have a son doesn't change things. Yes, I also wish Christopher were eight years old again—or better yet, a toddler, since I missed a lot of his early years by working too hard and letting Joanna raise him."

Realizing where they were, Tamara suggested, "Why don't we continue our conversation in the car?"

Bronson put his arm around her while they waited for the valet to bring the car around.

Tamara gave Bronson the keys, and he took Lincoln Avenue to Marine Drive, and then got on the expressway.

"So you feel guilty about not having spent more time with Christopher?"

"At the time, it seemed like the right thing to do. Mother stays home, father goes to work. I didn't realize I was cheating both myself and Joanna. If I hadn't imitated my father, who believed a woman's place was in the home, Joanna might not have felt so suffocated that she had to leave home to find herself."

Tamara looked at the Drake Hotel looming in the distance, the lights of Lake Shore Drive forming a diadem against the indigo-blue of the circling lake.

"You can't take all the blame. It wasn't right that she deserted her son."

Bronson glanced at her, and Tamara experienced goose bumps. If his just looking at her affected her this way, what would she feel if he made love to her?

She pushed the disturbing thought away, trying to concentrate on what Bronson was saying.

"No, but it's time I assumed some of the blame for being so inflexible. I used to lay all the guilt at my ex-wife's door, but now I see that I wasn't just the innocent, wronged party."

"I'm afraid I'm not that generous about my ex. Robert has not made an effort to see his daughter since she was six, and for that I'll never forgive him."

"Does he live in another state?"

"Oh, no. He's remarried, and still lives in Illinois. It's his choice not to make his daughter a part of his life."

As Lake Shore Drive veered sharply to the left, Bronson gave a right turn signal.

"How about driving through the Magnificent Mile before picking up Lake Shore Drive again?"

Tamara nodded happily. "Let's. I've always loved the Loop, and I worked on Wacker Drive a couple of summers while attending college. But I no longer have the patience to make this tortuous commute."

As they drove past the Hancock Center, and unique Water Tower, Tamara reflected anew at the affection Chicago inspired in its citizens.

"Do you follow soccer?" she asked suddenly.

Bronson smiled. "I used to play it in high school. And Christopher made me attend a few of the games when the World Cup opened up here this past summer."

"I attended one game—that's all I could manage," Tamara said with regret in her voice. "Sabrina and I were here for Venetian Night, when all the boats sailed amidst those wonderful fireworks, but I missed the opening parade."

"You can't be everywhere, Tamara," Bronson told her, his voice full of understanding. "Your main responsibility is to pay the bills and put food on the table—and you've done a wonderful job with Sabrina. If she chooses a wrong fork in the road, it's not your fault."

Tamara laughed shakily. "Boy, am I managing to spoil your evening. What a wet blanket. I guess mothers and guilt are inseparable twins."

"So operate and sever them," Bronson said harshly. "You don't deserve to tear yourself up over two immature ingrates."

"Yes, sir," Tamara said, laughing and feeling the tension seep away. "I hear you loud and clear."

The drive was magical. Tamara knew that no matter what happened in the future, she would always have this memory with Bronson.

She also felt somewhat vindicated. She *had* been taking a lot of blame on herself, vacillating between clearheaded thinking and maternal anguish.

But she had not forced her daughter to throw her future away. Sabrina was the one making the choices now, and if one of them meant that the future she had been working toward was going to hell in a handbasket . . . well, she was going to have to live with it.

It was Sabrina's life. Tamara was going to try to make her see the light.

Beyond that, she could not do any more.

Except always love Sabrina . . . and be there for her if and when she ever came to her senses.

Nine

It was 1:30 when Tamara and Bronson returned to the town house. Rather than leave the car in the front parking lot as she usually did during the week to save time, she asked Bronson to drive around the complex to park the Continental in the garage, which formed a communal, center island for all the residents.

Bronson had agreed to come in for coffee, because neither of them had wanted to cut the evening short, but both had realized Tamara could not relax with Sabrina alone in the house. It might be irrational, but after carrying her child for nine months, trying to anticipate every danger possible, and attempting to protect her daughter for almost eighteen years, Tamara realized she was not ready to totally let go. She had anticipated Sabrina being around for another four years at least, going to college.

Indeed, had she gone away to college, the separation might have been less painful, and provided a more gradual transition.

But the thought that Sabrina had been ready to cut all ties to her and disappear into the night with a young man Tamara barely knew had panicked her. Separation anxiety had become abject terror of abandonment and even worse, profound worry over Sabrina's lack of judgment and possible hard-luck future.

As Bronson and Tamara walked through the patio surrounded by privacy hedges and flowering trees, she grumbled, "I told Sabrina to keep the outside lights on. When will that child ever listen?"

"In her rebellious mode, I doubt she will listen to much of anything," Bronson said, putting his arm about her waist and squeezing reassuringly.

Although it was a Saturday night, and many people in Willowbrook Court—quite a few of them parents of teenagers attending Deerbrook High—stayed up late, Tamara always made it a practice to keep the volume down after ten, no matter what the circumstance. It had often proven a chore, when Sabrina had friends over or decided to play her stereo loud enough to wake the dead while studying for exams or to drown out any three-way conversations she might have on her phone. But Tamara strove to be a good neighbor.

With old-fashioned courtesy, Bronson took the house key from her and inserted it into the lock on the French door. Tamara led the way into the kitchen, trying to avoid making any noise so as not to wake Sabrina.

But giggling, coming from the direction of the living room, made her pause in midstride, and Bronson bumped into her from behind.

Tamara felt his thighs brush against her bottom, and his arms automatically came around her to steady her. She hoped her gulp was not audible, as the feel of his heavily muscled legs seemed to leave a burning imprint on her behind. His body seemed to mold itself to hers perfectly, and his arms felt strong and secure . . . and deliciously treacherous, both a warm haven and dangerous whirlpool.

Fighting the insidiously pleasant sensations coursing through her veins and turning her mind to mush, Tamara moved forward, and Bronson let his hands drop.

Tamara walked soundlessly through the dining room in the dark, the thick gray carpet muffling her steps, and unerringly found the living-room switch. With one flick, the room was flooded with light, and the two teenagers on the couch jumped apart as if jerked by a live wire.

"No wonder you weren't scared," Tamara said, surprised her voice came out so calm and reasonable.

Sabrina was too shocked and guilty to say anything, but Christopher leapt to his feet as Bronson came into view.

"Dad, what are *you* doing here?"

"Shouldn't I be asking *you* that?" Bronson said, his tone self-contained.

Inwardly, Tamara was relieved that Sabrina had had company. Also, finding Christopher and her daughter making out on the living room couch was a lot more reassuring than finding them in Sabrina's bedroom would have been.

"Mom, I didn't ask Christopher over until after you called, honest," Sabrina said, closing the top buttons on her lacy blouse with trembling fingers.

That in itself was a shock—seeing Sabrina in something other than sweat suits or a grunge look. The cynical, hurt part of her reflected that, of course, those tiny, rhinestone buttons provided a great turn-on, and were certainly fun and convenient to open up.

But Tamara refused to act like an uptight mother. Just because her child was metamorphosing into a sexual being—overnight, it seemed—before her very eyes, did not mean she had to act like a prude.

"You know how I feel about you lying," Tamara told her daughter, her voice acquiring a harsher tone.

Sabrina had been doing a lot of that lately—and it was the one thing that Tamara found hardest to forgive.

"It's true, Mrs. Hayward. Sabrina called me only a little while ago. She said that you'd called her, and that she began to feel afraid of being in the house alone."

Tamara did not believe *that* ruse for a minute. Like most teens, Sabrina considered herself immortal and immune to danger. "Why didn't you call Meghan, then? I asked you if you wanted to spend the night at her house, or some other friend's, or if you wanted to have someone over."

"Meghan and I are finished," Sabrina said with such teenage fervor that Tamara chose to let it pass—for the moment.

"And how did you get here?" Bronson said, taking off his tuxedo and loosening his shirt.

Tamara found her eyes following his every sexy movement with fascination, and had to recall herself to her surroundings and circumstances.

"Jonathan drove me over," Christopher said defiantly. "Unlike Meghan, Jonathan is a true friend."

"Oh, is he?" Bronson said with deceptive softness. "Say you two had gotten hitched, or Sabrina had—God forbid—gotten pregnant, and neither of you finished high school and had to make it on the outside world as dropouts. Would St. Jonathan be there to pick up the pieces ... and not just for one night, or a week?"

Christopher and Sabrina looked at each other, and Tamara could just read their hormone-laden minds. *Parents! What do they know of true love? What do they know of anything?*

"Well, Christopher, since you can't seem to tear yourself away from the fair Sabrina, and likewise for the young lady, and since both Tamara and I know that nothing we say will make a dent in your sexual drive, I guess you can join us for a bit of chaperoned companionship."

Sabrina and Christopher, who had looked uncomfortable as Bronson had mentioned the unmentionable, S-E-X, in mixed company—meaning cool kids and square fogies—stared at him as if he had lost his mind.

"What do you mean 'chaperoned companionship'?" Christopher asked suspiciously.

"I think your father means that if this were another century altogether, we parents would not be subjected to heart attacks and ulcers brought about by teenage promiscuity, with its dire consequences like pregnancy, AIDS, and other sexually transmitted diseases. Society would have made it a lot harder for you two to be together without adult supervision." Sighing, Tamara added, "But the age of the automobile and changing mores have made it harder on us relics. So, since you two cannot stand to be apart, you can join us."

The two kids looked at each other, then at Tamara and Bronson as if they had grown three heads.

"Are you feeling all right, Mother?" Sabrina asked in an adult tone. "It seems you've been working too hard."

Tamara took off her shawl, threw it in the direction of a chair, and removed her high-heeled strap sandals.

"And of course, with your typical solicitude, you've been helping me avoid overwork these past few years by cooking for me, doing the dishes, doing chores around the house—"

"You know I had a lot of homework, Mother!" Sabrina said indignantly, watching with horrified fascination as Tamara moved between Christopher and herself and sat on the very couch they had been putting to such enthusiastic use only minutes ago. "And I also spent hours and hours in practice, not to mention all those weekends I spent playing tournaments."

"Then I guess we've both sacrificed, haven't we?" Tamara said calmly, leaning back against the couch and crossing her legs. "In benefit of what I thought was a common goal—to get you into the best college possible, and into the best tennis program available.''

"There you go again, Mother," Sabrina said, looking down at her mother with unconcealed hostility. "I told you things have changed."

"Oh, I realize that," Tamara said, refusing to be baited this evening. She was still feeling mellow from tonight's lovely affair and Bronson's intoxicating company.

"Perhaps I have pushed you in the wrong direction. Your agenda now includes only Christopher, but you've lost the most important part: Sabrina. The vibrant, vital teenager I once knew is gone, replaced by a Stepford wife." Before Sabrina could retort, Tamara added, "I know, I know. We've already established it's *your* life. And you'll live it any way you see fit."

Tamara looked at Bronson and patted the couch next to her. "Would you like to see a movie? We're partial to horror around here, and our library is fully stocked with disgusting, totally violent fare."

"Don't mind if I do," Bronson said, draping his jacket over the back of a mauve chair and sitting down next to Tamara.

"Sabrina, dear, could you and Christopher put on some coffee and make some popcorn? With butter?"

She looked inquiringly at Bronson, who said, "Lots of butter."

Christopher and Sabrina stood on either side of them like department-store dummies. Tamara caught them exchanging puzzled, confused glances, and smiled inwardly. It was about time *they* experienced some uncertainty.

"What movie do you feel like seeing, Sabrina?"

"None, Mother," Sabrina said. "I'm actually feeling kind of tired."

"Oh, but you didn't look or sound tired just a minute ago, dear. How about *The Thing*?"

"Whatever, Mother," Sabrina said, flouncing out of the living room with Christopher hot on her heels.

Bronson looked down at her, and his gaze was alight with laughter. "Way to go, Mom. Turnabout is fair play."

"Oh, I've no doubt Sabrina is going to find some way to pay me back."

Bronson shrugged unconcernedly. "I think they're too busy marshaling their defenses to try an offensive right now." Putting his arm about her shoulders, he whispered, "I *am* sorry, though, that the house is occupied, especially with our offspring. I think Christopher had the right idea."

Tamara laughed throatily, letting her head rest on Bronson's shoulder.

"Mr. Kensington, I can see where Christopher gets his Don Juan tendencies."

"I don't fault his taste," Bronson said, his gaze alighting on her mouth and remaining there.

Tamara licked suddenly dry lips, and Bronson's gaze darkened. The arm about her shoulders became rock-solid, and his head inclined toward hers.

As Bronson's lips were about to meet Tamara's, Sabrina's voice, coming loud and clear from the direction of the kitchen, rudely interrupted his motion. "Mother, once I'm done with the popcorn, can I go to bed? I'm *absolutely* exhausted."

"We so seldom see each other lately, Sabrina," Tamara managed to counter in a reasonably level tone. Her chest swelled under the anticipation of the moment, and when Bronson's gaze dropped to her heaving bosom, Tamara ceased breathing altogether. "We'd love for you two to join us."

Tamara could hear the two teens whispering fiercely in the kitchen, but her whole concentration was centered on Bronson. She craved, yet dreaded, his kiss.

As he eliminated the distance between them, and his dark head blotted the light, Tamara closed her eyes and felt a moan rise from deep within her.

Bronson's mouth claimed hers and swallowed her note of need, and Tamara blindly turned to him, putting both her hands on his chest, wanting to feel his heat, his heartbeat, his closeness.

The kiss was far too short...yet it promised more, a lot more.

Tamara opened her eyes and felt her insides melt at the glittering look in Bronson's blue gray gaze. His cheeks were flushed, and his breathing quickened.

He inclined his head once more and kissed her eyes closed, his lips gossamer-soft against her eyelashes. Tamara felt as if she were dissolving, and would never be able to put herself together again. Knowing that the kids were in an adjacent room did nothing to diminish her longing.

When Bronson moved away from her, putting some much-needed distance between them, she felt cold and bereft.

How had this happened? How could it have happened so fast?

Granted, she had not led a life of wild, sexual encounters, but until meeting Bronson, she had not even felt her social life lacking.

They were supposed to be solving their children's problems, not borrowing some of their own.

Her questioning glance met Bronson's, but she read no answers there. Only an echoing yearning that matched her own.

Oh, boy!

The clanking and clinking from the kitchen brought her to her senses—halfway, at least.

Tamara tried to sit up on the couch, but found that her bones had melted, and her spine seemed liquid. With effort, she managed to look composed when Sabrina and Christopher appeared with the coffee and popcorn.

"Sabrina, would you please get the movie?"

"The more recent version, right? John Carpenter's, with Kurt Russell?"

Tamara looked at Bronson, glad to have something mundane to talk about.

"Which one would you like to see—the fifties original, or the eighties version?"

"Oh, by all means, the original," Bronson said.

"Oh, come on, Dad," Christopher complained. "That one is so lame."

"What do you expect from two doddering old fools, son?" Bronson said.

Christopher glanced at Sabrina, at his father, then back at Sabrina again. Christopher's look of disgust, shared by Sabrina, said it all.

Without a word, Sabrina got the older version from their library of videos and stuffed it into the VCR with little gentleness.

"Why don't you bring some plates, Sabrina, so we can all have some popcorn?"

"We don't touch butter, Mother," Sabrina said with virtuous disdain.

"Suit yourself," Tamara said unconcernedly, digging into the popcorn with relish. "Please turn off the light."

Bronson let his hand rest on her shoulder, where his fingers periodically caressed it.

Sabrina glared at Bronson's position on the couch, but Bronson ignored her pointed looks, as well as Christopher's.

The two teenagers took chairs at opposite ends of the room, and gave loud, simultaneous sighs at being forced to watch such a geeky show.

Not too long into the movie, though, Sabrina and Christopher sank to the floor in front of the couch, and unconsciously came closer together until they were lying shoulder to shoulder.

Tamara and Bronson exchanged amused glances in the gloom, and Bronson dropped a quick kiss on Tamara's mouth, which left her body clamoring for more.

Her hand instinctively sought his thigh and rested there, while Bronson's fingers gently massaged the tension out of her neck.

Although the kids became engrossed in the Arctic world of danger and suspense despite themselves, Tamara knew she and Bronson did not catch all of the movie.

By the end of the video, Tamara was heartily seconding Bronson's desire to have the house to themselves. . . .

Ten

Hostilities in the Hayward household escalated even further the following morning.

Sabrina slammed the raisin bran on the oval kitchen table, then slammed the refrigerator door after getting her low-fat milk, and then scraped her chair across the floor before settling down, in a way she knew was bound to irritate her mother.

"Finished with the histrionics?" Tamara asked, striving to maintain some semblance of serenity.

"Oh, I see," Sabrina said with utmost disdain. "Whatever *you* feel is legitimate and adult, and what *I* feel is just theatrical, not real at all?"

Tamara sensed the hurt underneath the bravado and tried to take her daughter's hand in hers. Sabrina snatched it away and put her hands on her lap.

"I'm sorry if we gave you the impression—"

"That's another thing, Mother," Sabrina interrupted heatedly. "What's all this 'we' stuff? It used to be just the two of us."

Sabrina realized her tactical mistake immediately, but Tamara jumped in before she could correct herself.

"That's exactly what I've been talking about, Sabrina. It *had* been just the two of us. We were so close, and we shared everything. That's why I'm so hurt... because you never confided in me and snuck behind my back."

She raised her hand when Sabrina opened her mouth to object. "Hear me out. We'll discuss things one more time— and then it's up to you to decide, once and for all."

Sabrina looked positively mutinous, but Tamara ignored the melodramatics. "I never meant to make light of your feelings. Certainly they're valid and real. First love can be intense and wonderful—but it can also bring untold dangers. First of all, your body is growing, and you don't have control over your emotions..."

"I know, I know," Sabrina muttered. "Heard all about it in Health 101."

"Well, then you know that your body sometimes gets ahead of your mind and judgment—and certainly ahead of your experience. You're not equipped to deal with all the complications and complexities of love—or sex. That's why adults try to protect their children. Believe it or not, parents were young once, too, and felt this way themselves."

Absently pouring cereal into her oversize bowl, Sabrina asked, "Then if you survived, why can't you trust me to do the same?"

Tamara toyed with her English muffin. "Because we're not talking just about survival. We're talking about living a full, enriched, satisfying life."

"Hasn't your life been satisfying?" Sabrina asked, pausing in the act of drowning her cereal with milk.

"Yes, it has. Up to a point. Your father and I met in college, and I had always wanted to go for my master's right after getting my bachelor's. Like you, I graduated a year early, and it wouldn't have killed your father to wait another eighteen months—I was willing to go to school year-round again. But he told me to choose...him or my education. I chose him—and I've lived to regret it."

"But you've done okay," Sabrina insisted.

"But you don't know at what price," Tamara said, putting some apricot jelly on her muffin. "After he did that disappearing act from your life, I had to be both mother and father. Of necessity, my needs had to come second, and my visions of a challenging, leisurely degree were gone. I had to work long hours, *and* go to school at night. Since Grandma and Grandpa died when I was a senior in high school, you didn't even have a grandmother who could baby-sit you. I agonized when I had to leave you with relative strangers...when all I wanted was to be there for you, each and every second of your life."

"But I turned out all right," Sabrina said, munching on her cereal.

"And that says a lot about your character and determination," Tamara said, fighting back tears. She had to keep control. Sabrina hated to see her cry. All teenagers were turned off by waterworks, but her daughter was especially resistant to emotionalism on Tamara's part. "But I still missed out on a lot. Children grow up so fast, and I wasn't always there when you said a new word, or didn't feel well, or learned a new game. I wanted to teach you everything, take care of every fever and sniffle and tummyache, witness each and every smile and nuance of your growing up."

Sabrina reflected on her mother's words. Tamara took a small bite out of her muffin, which she ordinarily enjoyed. But today the sourdough muffin tasted like sawdust.

"So, if I have a kid, I'll just stay home. By then, Christopher will be established—"

"But that's just it, honey," Tamara said gently. "It will take many years for Christopher to get established. He's not ready to turn pro, and even if he gets to that stage—and if he gets some assistance from the USTA rookie touring program, in itself highly unlikely, it'll take quite a while to climb through the rankings. It's like the minor leagues in baseball."

"So, we'll just wait to have children," Sabrina said stubbornly.

"That can't always be helped—"

"I told you, Mother, Christopher and I haven't had sex yet!"

"But it won't be long. The feelings you two have for each other are strong, and so are the needs of your young, healthy bodies. You have to guard against it—"

"You sound like we have a disease—"

"You could get one, yes. And don't forget, no birth control is one-hundred-percent effective. How are you going to work if you have a baby? Who will support whom? You couldn't travel with Christopher all over the country, let alone overseas. Especially with a baby."

"You're just assuming I'm going to get pregnant, aren't you?" Sabrina said, her chin raised pugnaciously. "I thought you looked forward to grandchildren."

"Down the road, Sabrina. I'd love to have them, but only after you've gotten your education, seen a bit of of the world, experienced life, gotten situated—"

"What's this obsession you have about an education, Mother?" Sabrina asked, reopening the cereal box and picking out some more raisins.

Tamara was caught between amusement over this sign of Sabrina's child-woman personality, and poignancy over the fact that the woman was on the verge of fully emerging, and her child on the edge of disappearing. Forever.

"Because nowadays, with the economy the way it is, a college degree is almost what a high-school degree was twenty years ago. And even college graduates have to take entry-level jobs like bank clerks that underpay and under-utilize their skills and knowledge.''

"So...what's the difference?" Sabrina asked, pouring herself some more grapefruit juice. "I can also get a job at a bank—I've had business courses.''

"The point is, Sabrina, that when the possibility for promotion comes up, the college grad will be considered first.'' Tamara took a sip of her coffee and found it lukewarm. "And we're talking about your gifts here, your intelligence. There's nothing sadder than a mind wasted, and a potential, whether musical, athletic or academic, going unfulfilled.''

"There you go again, Mother. We're back to my turning pro.''

"It's what you've worked toward for eleven long years. Now you can see the light at the end of the tunnel—''

"Which for me is the train, Mother! I told you, all those old plans are gone. And if I change my mind, I can always turn pro later, or get a degree—''

"Once you're out of the loop, it's hard to get back into it. Many people never make it back to college,'' Tamara said, taking another sip of her cold coffee and grimacing. "As for turning pro, it's harder on women to wait, since they develop sooner. If you stop playing now, it would take you a long time to regain your form—and your competitive edge.''

Sabrina mulled over her mother's words while she drank some more juice. "All right, how about this? I'll go to my practices this week, and I'll play the remaining meets and invitational, to make sure DHS gets into state. And you lay off Christopher and me.''

Tamara shook her head, her heart and head hurting. "Sabrina, haven't you heard a word I've said? I'm not trying to barter or haggle with you. I'm trying to help you envision a future in which hardship looms...and what's worse, a future in which you'll spend your days crying over what's been lost to you, over the things you didn't do.''

"I know, I know," Sabrina said impatiently. "You told me how people regret the things they haven't accomplished more than the things they shouldn't have done. But you seem to forget that this is *my* future we're talking about, and that I'm the one who has to decide. And I'm not *you*, Mother."

"I think that's unfair, and uncalled for, Sabrina," Tamara said, abandoning all hope of finishing her coffee. She was also beginning to lose hope over Sabrina ever seeing the light. "I gave you every chance to be what *you* wanted. You took guitar and piano lessons—at which you excelled—and you tried swimming, ice-skating, karate, soccer, gymnastics, basketball, baseball...everything under the sun. You've always been a very good student, and you're so talented in everything, academics, music, athletics—"

"And don't you think that puts a lot of pressure on me, Mother?" Sabrina said, toying with the condensation on her glass of grapefruit juice.

"I know it does, Sabrina. But the pressure has not come from me. I've only made it possible for you to try as many things as possible, because I want you to have a full life. The motivation and pressure has to come from you, Sabrina. Don't forget, I've raised you, and I know that sooner or later you'll regret not making the best of yourself that you can be—"

"Recruiting for the Marines now, Mother?" Sabrina said, getting up.

Tamara knew the conversation was over, and she felt frustrated. It seemed everything she'd said had gone over her daughter's head. She should not have been surprised, though. At Sabrina's age, the only advice that counted was that of her peers—parents were expendable, something to be suffered and tolerated.

Tamara remained seated and hid her hands in her lap. Her nails were digging into her palms to prevent her from screaming at the futility of it all. Why couldn't she prevent the disaster she saw looming? Why couldn't she get a time machine that she could run forward, and show Sabrina what was coming? Barring that, why couldn't she take on all the pain and disappointment and regret that loomed on her child's horizon?

"One last word, Sabrina," Tamara said quietly. "And then we'll shelve the subject. I realize this is your life. But will you at least promise me that you'll think back over the past seventeen years, and reflect over what you've been trying to accomplish? Having a boyfriend doesn't mean that you have to give up yourself, your sense of self. Please hang on to your dreams, and don't sell yourself short."

"My dreams have changed, Mother," Sabrina said with finality as she picked up her bowl and glass and took it to the sink. "We've discussed this over and over again, and I've given you a chance to have your say. But my mind's made up. I want Christopher—and you can't stop me."

Sabrina's last words echoed angrily in the kitchen as she ran upstairs to her room—no doubt to call Christopher and regale him with the excruciating, totally unreal discussion her mother had forced on her. Tamara resisted the urge to put her head down on the table and cry. She knew that if she did, she'd never stop.

Telling herself that she'd done the best she could do and the rest was up to Sabrina, Tamara took the remaining dishes to the sink. She started to wash them, then caught herself. Calling to her daughter to clean the kitchen, Tamara went into her study to continue work on two new clients. But she found it hard to concentrate. Thoughts of Bronson kept intruding and she had to use all her willpower to remain at her computer,

She really wished Bronson were with her...and for a lot more than moral support.

That evening, Bronson called. Tamara was glad for the interruption. She needed contact with another adult, especially one who had an idea of what she was going through. The sound of his voice was the next best thing to his being there.

"Christopher told me about your discussion with Sabrina."

Tamara chuckled. "So what were his sentiments? Let's burn the witch at the stake? Or boil the ogre in oil?"

"He told me in no uncertain terms that you should stop torturing Sabrina and trying to come between them or face the consequences."

"That's what terrifies me. The fact that they don't see the land mines ahead, and the consequences of their hormonally driven actions."

"We shouldn't throw stones," Bronson reminded her gently. "*Our* hormones are not exactly in hibernation."

"I know." Tamara sighed. "And he doesn't have to worry about further torture. I've said everything I had to say. The rest is up to them."

"Well, it's easier for Sabrina, really," Bronson said in a consoling tone. "Christopher is the one who really has to come to a decision. As the breadwinner—"

"What did you say?" Tamara interrupted, thinking she'd not heard right.

"Christopher is the one who stands to lose the most," Bronson said. Tamara could hear the puzzled note in his tone, and his obtuseness further infuriated her. "He's the one who really needs the college degree, and he's the one most likely to turn pro, so it stands to reason—"

"Can he get pregnant?" Tamara asked with deceptive softness.

"No, of course not. But I'm sure the kids are smart enough to take precautions and—"

"*I* took precautions," Tamara said. "Precautions don't always work—and I was married, and at least had a degree."

"So, if worst comes to worst, they could get married. I'd be willing to help if a grandchild came along—"

"I'm sure that's what they are counting on, and why they are not dealing with reality. But I'll be damned if I'll be a party to this. If it's *their* life and *their* decision, then they can damn well make it on their own!" Tamara said angrily. "And you seem to have overlooked something. What about Sabrina?"

"Christopher says she doesn't mind waiting to get her college education. And if she's willing to give up the idea of turning pro—"

"And stand aside? And leave the field open and clear to your darling son? It's obvious here who's the one truly in love and willing the make the ultimate sacrifice."

"What do you mean 'ultimate'? Sabrina loves Christopher, and my son loves your daughter. These are adjustments they'll both have to make."

"Yes, and Sabrina will be making them, while your son the prince will magnanimously accept them."

The wires crackled with tension. It was obvious that dense Bronson had finally realized she was mad. More than that, royally incensed.

"You're not being reasonable, Tamara. Listen to yourself. Just because you had an unplanned, unwanted pregnancy—"

"How dare you! Sabrina might have been unplanned, but she was *never* unwanted," Tamara said fiercely, belatedly lowering her voice. She knew Sabrina was up in her room studying, since she'd been grounded for a week as a result of her escapades. Tamara might have made it longer, but she knew Homecoming was fast approaching, and she did not want to keep her daughter from her last official school event, and the last dance of her high-school career. Since she was graduating in seven semesters, instead of the traditional eight, she would not be around for the prom. Unless she and Christopher saw the light.

"Be that as it may, it's obvious you have some unresolved feelings about your marriage and divorce. But that is neither here nor there. The important thing—"

"Is your precious son, right?" Tamara felt fury choke her. "Things don't really change, do they? Girls still come in last. Well, I'll have you know Sabrina is *not* a second-class citizen, and her future is just as important as your boy's. She certainly has a lot more to lose—and if you don't see that, there's no use in us discussing this any further."

Her hands trembling, Tamara replaced the receiver gently—then unplugged the phone. If Sabrina wanted to talk to Christopher, tough. She'd had enough of the Kensingtons to last her a lifetime....

Eleven

Tamara locked the door to her office and breathed in the fresh October night air. She loved autumn, and she loved the small shopping center her company was located in. The businesses were all situated in remodeled town houses, which gave the complex a homey feeling. The winter-white bricks with their variously shaded shutters dispelled any feeling of uniformity, as did the different signs with their unique shapes and coloring. But the whole ambience made customers think of the businesses as trusted friends.

Hayward Sports Consulting was sandwiched between Great Benefits Insurance—GBI—and Davidson Sportsmedicine. Tamara smiled, thinking that clients had an all-purpose group here. You could insure yourself against accidents or illness, consult with Tamara about the latest on science, nutrition and sports psychology, and—should worst come to worst—get rehabbed and back to normal at Davidson's.

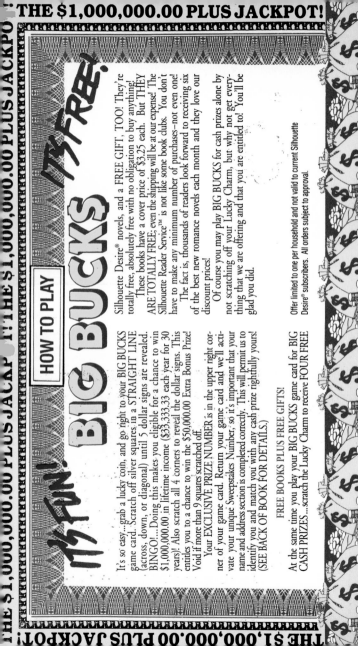

EXCLUSIVE PRIZE # 3L 771323

BIG BUCKS

$

TWO
WAYS
TO WIN
BIG
BUCKS!

1. Uncover 5 $ signs in a row... BINGO! You're eligible for a chance to win the $1,000,000.00 SWEEPSTAKES!

2. Uncover 5 $ signs in a row AND uncover $ signs in all 4 corners... BINGO! You're also eligible for a chance to win the $50,000.00 EXTRA BONUS PRIZE!

LUCKY CHARM GAME!

Claim 4 FREE Books AND a FREE Mystery Gift!

Hurry!
This jackpot must be claimed!
Scratch here ↗

YES! I have played my BIG BUCKS game card as instructed. Enter my Big Bucks Prize number in the MILLION DOLLAR Sweepstakes III and also enter me for the Extra Bonus Prize. When winners are selected, tell me if I've won. If the Lucky Charm is scratched off, I will also receive everything revealed, as explained on the back of this page.

225 CIS AS3M
(U-SIL-D-07/95)

NAME _____

ADDRESS _____ APT. _____

CITY _____ STATE _____ ZIP _____

Gathering her wool car coat closer against the night wind, Tamara put her briefcase under her arm and held on to the black-and-gray railing as she descended the few steps to the sidewalk and the diagonal parking lot. The cluster of buildings was set back from the street, which also contributed to the residential, friendly feeling.

She almost pitched down the stairs headfirst when a deep voice reached her from below.

"Have you had dinner yet?"

"Good evening, Mr. Kensington," Tamara said with a coolness that eclipsed the crisp nocturnal breeze.

She descended the last two steps, approached her car and inserted the key in the lock. But before she could open the door, Bronson leaned against it.

"I'd like to apologize," he said softly.

Tamara's nostrils flared. She was torn between fury at his cavalier attitude and self-condemnation at her treacherous response to his nearness and the distinctive woodsy smell of his cologne.

About to tell him to move away from her car, she found her directive sabotaged as he dropped a kiss on her nose.

"You have the sexiest twitching since 'Bewitched,'" he told her, looking amused and aroused.

Tamara was aroused, all right—but not amused.

"And you have some unmitigated gall. What gives you the right to come over to my place of employment and harass me?"

"I knew that if I tried to call you on the phone, you'd hang up on me. Heck, *I'd* hang up on me, too. I acted like a real jerk."

Tamara toyed with her keys, trying to regain her composure. She'd known Bronson would be trouble as soon as she'd seen him.

Of course, her overzealous hormones were not too broken up about Bronson showing up.

"Your acting like a jerk seems to be somewhat of a character pattern."

"I know. I'm deeply flawed. Here I'd thought I was a liberated male until my son's welfare stood in the balance."

Bronson's hands lifted her short camel-colored coat and slipped about her waist. He propelled her toward him, and whispered against her lips, "Am I forgiven?"

Knowing how tempted she was to say yes, Tamara pushed against his chest. Her hands remained there, liking the strong, warm feel of him and the solid thudding of his heartbeat.

She might be in the prime of her life, and it might have been a long time since she'd had a satisfying sexual relationship, but she was not seventeen. Sabrina was, and she needed a mother who could show a modicum of self-control under such tantalizing circumstances.

"Not yet. Why is it that men always think sex can solve everything?"

"Because it can help *a lot* of things," Bronson said, his hands moving upward from her waist and caressing her back. "In my case, making love with you could ease this deep ache I feel."

His husky tone sent shivers up her back, which the provoking touch of his experienced fingers magnified.

"In my case, I do not make out in the middle of the street like a sex-starved teenager." Tamara conveniently ignored the fact that she was a sex-starved adult—at least where this man was concerned. "Secondly, I'm not a young thing who's going to be easily seduced by pretty words. Thirdly, if you're in such pain, I suggest you take a cold shower—or resolve your urgent need in the privacy of your own bedroom."

"Ouch!" Bronson said, chuckling as Tamara shoved vigorously against his chest, this time resisting the ambrosial sensations his nearness engendered. "You really go for the jugular."

"If you're going to act juvenile, then you should use juvenile solutions," Tamara said briskly as she opened her car door. "And as for the jugular, you should know how mothers are when they defend their young."

"I thought you and I were in this together," Bronson said, leaning against the door as she turned on the ignition and lowered the driver's window.

"I thought so too, until you put your son's future ahead of *my* child's."

"What we have to realize is that our kids seem determined to entwine their futures, and we have to find a way to reconcile everyone's needs."

Tamara knew Bronson was referring to more than their kids' situation. But right now, she had to keep a clear head, and giving in to her natural inclination and desire was not the path to lucid behavior.

"I agree." Seeing how the night wind was whipping Bronson's thick, dark hair about reminded her that he was exposed to the elements, with only his navy blue jacket and thin shirt to guard against the cold.

"You'd better get in your car. We need to be healthy to deal with this crisis, or our kids will wear us down even sooner."

"So how about dinner?"

"Not tonight," Tamara said politely. "I'm meeting a client early tomorrow morning, and I have some work to finish yet. I'm going home now only to make sure Sabrina is where she's supposed to be—in her room."

"Christopher said Sabrina's grounded, and not taking her 'untenable position' too well."

"She's lucky I didn't ground her longer. But with Homecoming coming up—"

"—and Sabrina out of high school in just a few weeks, you didn't want to shortchange her," Bronson said, his eyes gleaming with understanding and banked desire.

Tamara nodded. "I'd better get going. I've been driving Sabrina to and from school—which she deeply resents—and it's been cutting even more into my available time."

"What about later in the week?" Bronson asked as he straightened.

A sudden gust blew Bronson's jacket away from his body, and Tamara got a clear view of his light blue shirt, which did a phenomenal job of adhering to his muscular chest and narrow waist.

Licking suddenly dry lips, Tamara told herself she'd better get away from Bronson, and fast. The Kensington men were really trouble. How could she blame Sabrina for her infatuation with the younger, when she was not far from falling for the elder?

Do as I say, not as I do?

"We'll see," Tamara told him. "I'd better get home before Sabrina starves to death."

She could see Bronson staring after her as she drove away.

"Hey, Dad, when is Sabrina going to be let out of jail?"

Bronson walked into the living room, loosened his tie, and took off his jacket, which he hung over the back of an armchair. Although he preached to his son daily regarding the necessity of neatness and hanging up one's clothes, he knew he was not making much of an impression on Christopher. And tonight he didn't have the energy to get into it with his son. His thoughts were on Tamara. It had been a long time since a woman had kept him going in circles...and he didn't like the uncertain sensation.

"Did you hear me, Dad? Sabrina's incarcerated in that damned town house, and her warden drives her to and from school every day. She's going crazy being cooped up like that."

"You should have thought of that before you ran away with Sabrina and rented a motel room," Bronson said wearily as he dropped onto the couch. He'd looked forward to some peace and quiet, but it never failed. He was forever trying to get Christopher to open up, with his son running away from a friendly, natural interest as if it were the Spanish Inquisition.

Tonight, when Bronson wanted to sit in the dark and ponder the enigmatic Ms. Hayward, his son was in an effusive mood. Or rather, a squawky mode.

"Aren't we ever going to be able to live that down, Dad?" Christopher said, aiming himself like a missile at a chair that groaned under his weight and putting his size thirteen sneakers on the arm of the abused furniture. "It's not like Bree and me are thirteen. I'm of age, and she will be too, soon."

Even the offensive feet and wrong pronoun were not enough to goad Bronson. He concentrated on the more immediate, urgent matter.

"You and Sabrina are going to have to earn our trust, Chris. You always had it, and neither Sabrina's mother nor I ever thought you two could lie and betray us the way you did."

"When did we lie, Dad? You weren't around—"

"Can the guilt trip, Chris. Believe me, I blame myself enough already. But I also know I did the best I could, and you can't look me in the eye and tell me you ever doubted the fact that I love you." Bronson noticed Christopher squirming. Teenage boys might be real macho dudes when it came to their girlfriends, but the concept of love coming from a parent made them itchier than poison ivy. "As you said, both of you are old enough to know better. Therefore, you should have been more responsible. And if you really love Sabrina as much as you claim you do, then you'd never have put her in such a situation."

"Oh, come on, don't start on that reputation thing again. I had to hear enough from Brandy—and here I thought that she was cool, and not living in some Victorian dark age."

"Brandy is one of the most modern, intelligent women I know. And the double standard's still alive and well, unfortunately. When you love someone, you try to protect her, whether it's from whispers in school when gossip gets around, or from the possibility of pregnancy or the loss of her education."

"I told you, Dad," Christopher said impatiently. "We haven't done it yet. There's *no way* she could get pregnant."

"Are you telling me you and Sabrina haven't been making love at all? Going pretty far? Aren't you feeling sorry for yourself because Sabrina has had the sense not to give in yet?"

Christopher blushed, and Bronson had to make an effort not to smile. His son might act studly, but he knew that deep down, the boy was sensitive. He just hoped that, for both their sakes, and particularly Sabrina's, Christopher continued to exercise the restraint he'd shown so far.

Dropping his legs to the floor and his eyes to the gold carpeting, Christopher said, "You know, Dad . . ."

Bronson waited for his son to continue. He tiredly rubbed the back of his neck, regretting, not for the first time, that he was not married. If only he didn't have to face all these parental mine fields alone!

"You promise not to laugh?"

"You know me better than that, son. How could I ever laugh about any honest, sincere emotion you have, let alone something as important as this?"

Christopher's face was obscured, but the tips of his ears were burning red.

"I'm afraid—I'm afraid—"

When Christopher gulped, and seemed stuck, Bronson said encouragingly, "Yes?"

"I guess I must sound like a real first-class wuss, but I'm afraid of disappointing Sabrina."

The last words, muffled since Christopher had his chin tucked into his chest, came out in a rush. Slowly, Christopher raised his gaze to meet his father's.

Bronson felt his eyes burning, but made a heroic effort not to reveal how affected he was by his son's statement.

"I'd say your comment indicates the exact opposite, Chris. It tells me that you are really becoming a man."

Christopher sat up a bit straighter, and his expression grew interested. "How so?"

"Because there's a lot more to sex than erection and ejection."

"Oh, Dad!" Christopher said, moving in the chair as if he were ready to bolt.

"Hear me out!" Bronson's calm command kept his son glued to his seat. "There's more to sex than mechanics, and that's what we talked about when you were ten and began asking questions in earnest. I guess I should have concentrated more on the emotional side of things."

"That's all right, Dad," Christopher said in an embarrassed tone. "I guess I wouldn't have been ready to hear about responsibility and birth-control methods just then."

"What exactly is worrying you about having sex with Sabrina? Why are you afraid you'll disappoint her?"

Christopher looked away, up and down and all around, and finally, reluctantly, let his gaze meet his father's. "Because I'm crazy about her. I don't want to be Quick Draw McGraw. I don't want to be a dud-stud."

"I'm sure in Sabrina's eyes, that would be impossible. The thing to remember is, put her needs before yours."

"That's easier said than done. I've never loved anyone the way I love Bree, and I just don't know, if I start really going at it, really letting go, I don't know if—"

"You'll have a premature ejaculation?"

Bronson knew he was embarrassing the boy even more by using technical terms. But since they were discussing the girl he loved, the daughter of the woman he—Bronson pushed that unsettling thought to the back burner and concentrated on his son—street terms were not appropriate.

"Yeah. I guess so."

"Like I said, put her needs before yours. Make sure you engage in plenty of foreplay, and ask her if there's anything she likes."

"Like Sabrina's going to know. She has less experience than me."

"Don't sell girls short, Chris. Sabrina is almost a woman, and she's very intelligent and self-aware. She knows her own mind, she knows what she wants, and she wants *you*. I'm sure she won't have any problems letting you know if you're going too fast."

Christopher brightened. "You're right, Dad. Bree has often told me where to go. She doesn't take any junk—I mean, like you said, she has a mind of her own."

"Then it probably won't be any different in bed—when you get to that point."

Realizing that his son seemed to be absorbing his words, Bronson ventured some more advice. "Remember, Chris, if you decide against abstinence, make sure you practice safe sex. Protection is synonymous with affection."

Christopher's shoulders twitched, and Bronson knew it was time to let up. His son must really care for Sabrina a whole lot if he had subjected himself to some advice from the old man.

"The most important thing in lovemaking, which, after all, is just a part of the total package of your relationship, Chris, is caring and gentleness. Treasure Sabrina. Take care of her."

"Yeah, yeah," Christopher said, unfolding his long, lanky frame a foot at a time.

Christopher's huge strides took him toward the stairs and escape in record time.

"Oh, son. One more thing."

Christopher turned around, a suffering look on his face. "Just remember. Being aroused is never an excuse to force yourself on a girl, or to attempt to get her sympathy in order to get into her pants. Never try to manipulate a girl into saying yes, when she really means no."

"Dad, I'm not a rapist," Christopher said, his tone deeply aggrieved.

"I know, Chris. But blackmailing for sex through love isn't allowed either. What makes a man is knowing how to control himself."

Christopher looked offended for a few seconds, but then mulled over his father's words and nodded. "Got you, Dad. Thanks."

Bronson felt the unfamiliar stinging in his eyes return. Maybe he wasn't a complete failure.

No father could consider himself a total bust when his horny eighteen-year-old responded to advice on self-denial the way Christopher just had.

Maybe there *was* hope, after all. For both of them.

Twelve

The next few days left Tamara feeling exhausted.

She needed more help, now that word of mouth was spreading and her business expanding. Shelley, the college student she'd hired to come in four hours a day Monday through Saturday, had just informed her she'd have to cut down on either days or hours, since she was changing her major and needed to take additional courses in the next quarter.

Tamara was debating hiring a full-time employee, but dependable personnel who had the right skills and experience—knowing how to type, operate a computer, use a calculator, and deal with the public—were not easy to find.

Especially not at the hourly wage Tamara could afford to pay.

She knew Bronson wanted to get together to discuss strategy—although this was an obvious euphemism for other things he wanted—and she was looking forward to talking to him... about a lot of issues. Maybe she could discuss her business situation with him. After all, Bronson was a savvy executive who had just received an award for his business acumen. He could offer some suggestions and at the very least act as a sounding board.

Tamara felt virtuous about her decision. She decided to ignore the fact that she had gone into business for herself and had made a go of it long before meeting Bronson Kensington.

She was honest enough to admit that she was tired of making decisions—financial or personal. The knowledge that Sabrina's father lived nearby, and yet did not even attempt to see his daughter or be a part of her life, gnawed at her. Most of the time, she was able to put the frustration and anger out of her mind.

But now that she was faced with such serious issues as Sabrina's future—and possibly even her health—it would have been nice to have someone else with whom to shoulder the tremendous combined load of decision-making, uncertainty and responsibility.

Tamara had found being a single parent—fulfilling and meaningful as it was—to be the strongest challenge she'd faced.

"Hey, Mom. Are you coming to the meet tomorrow?"

Tamara glanced up from the figures she was analyzing in her ledgers and looked blankly at her suddenly amicable offspring.

Such congeniality brought instant distrust, but Tamara fought to keep it from her voice. "I thought you'd told me to stay away from your tennis tournaments and school matches. According to you, I've been smothering you and putting too much pressure on you just by being there." Privately Tamara had resented the ultimatum, since most of Sabrina's teammates appreciated their parents' presence, rare as those appearances were. Few mothers—and even fewer fathers—came to watch the girls play. Since her daughter's edict, Tamara had felt cut off from yet another aspect of Sabrina's life.

"Well, it's fun being able to drive my own car. Many of the kids in school are snobs, and a lot wealthier than us."

Tamara raised her eyebrows, but refrained from comment. Sabrina munched on a banana and swung a leg over the arm of a rocking chair. Tamara also refrained from reminding her daughter of both the danger and inelegance of her pose—Sabrina had tipped over a couple of times, suffering bruises and a sprain—and was proud of her self control.

"I know, I know," Sabrina said, wiping her hands on her gray school sweatpants. At least they weren't the expensive designer ones. "You told me that anyone who bases personal worth or friendship on bank balances isn't worth knowing. But still, it's really cool to drive my Mustang to the meets, and also to some of the junior tournaments."

"Which reminds me, you never did tell me how the Decatur event turned out," Tamara said leadingly.

"Well, you know how those Central Illinois tourneys are," Sabrina said vaguely. "But since you missed the meet Monday, I thought you might want to come to the one tomorrow afternoon. It's a home match, and we should be able to annihilate the Northfield Warriors."

"You mean they're going to play you against their number one? I thought they were a weak team, and your assistant coach wanted to offer some match experience to the other positions. And what about your sense of challenge? Didn't you used to look forward to tough matches, not mere walkovers?"

"Yeah, well," Sabrina said evasively, frowning. Apparently the conversation was not leading exactly where she wanted it to. And Tamara had a pretty good idea of its ultimate direction.

"I thought I could save you some time if you'd let me drive to school. Both in the morning and afternoon. That way I'd be right there for practice, and you wouldn't have to drive so far."

"You know I enjoy being with you, Sabrina. I never minded driving you around. And even though Monday was not a home game, there was no problem since you took the team bus to the away school."

"Does that mean you won't let me drive the car yet?"

Tamara set her books down and looked her daughter straight in the eye. "You may have the car for Saturday's away invitational—not before."

"But we all have to take the school bus. Ms. Cavanaugh said no exceptions, not even for seniors or co-captains," Sabrina wailed. "That's so totally unfair."

"Ms. Cavanaugh knows what she's doing. And what about your team spirit? I thought you liked being with your teammates."

"That was before," Sabrina mumbled, her lower lip jutting out.

"Before Christopher came to occupy one hundred percent of your mind—and activities. What about *you*, Sabrina? Don't you count for anything? Why abandon everything for your boyfriend? Is he asking you to?"

"Oh, Mother. You don't know Christopher. You won't even give him a chance." Sabrina jumped from the rocking chair, which flailed wildly about in danger of somersaulting before it righted itself. "You don't know *anything!*" she screamed as she ran out of the room.

Tamara took a deep breath. She resisted the impulse to follow Sabrina. Her daughter needed some cooling off. Tamara replayed their conversation and felt that she'd had the right to ask the questions she had. Kids were so used to chanting their right to privacy and independence like some holy mantra that oftentimes parents were intimidated, afraid of doing the wrong thing and irreparably damaging their precious ones' psyches.

Sabrina, though, was one tough cookie. And a smart one. Tamara decided she didn't have to feel any more guilty than usual: she'd tried to lay off, but she was not about to compromise on the grounding. There had to be some limits and consequences.

Of course, Tamara knew that the real reason Sabrina was upset was because she hadn't gotten her way—and her beloved car. Tamara had even begun to resent the invention of the automobile. She had come to hate the whole Industrial Revolution. How much easier it would be if children did not have cars to give them instant mobility and freedom—and such a private, convenient place to make out.

But she was certainly justified in asking her daughter some questions about her boyfriend. So far, she didn't know if Christopher shared Bronson's Neanderthal ideas about the man being the breadwinner and controlling partner in a relationship . . . or whether it was Sabrina who had gone off the deep end, forgetting all in the face of her reckless, youthful passion.

Tamara could almost laugh at the situation. It was almost a soap opera. Almost.

But there was nothing funny when one's own child was involved, and soap-opera solutions were not real life.

Tamara called Bronson, asking him if he wanted to come see Sabrina play. It would give them a chance to discuss some things.

But Bronson couldn't make it. He had an emergency at the factory, precipitated by the illness of his foreman. The molds and dies that were supposed to be ready this week were in danger of not being delivered in time. As it was, Bronson would have to cover two shifts every day this week.

Tamara wished him luck, and went to Sabrina's meet with trepidation. She wasn't sure whether she was still wanted, but she figured if she saw her daughter acting pained at her presence, she'd leave. Quickly and quietly.

Making her way to the top of one of the bleachers, Tamara stopped to converse a bit with some of the other mothers. She had never missed a meet or invitational during Sabrina's freshman or sophomore years, but when Sabrina became a junior, their relationship had altered. Sabrina became more moody and distant, dropping hints about her attendance, and then asking her not to show up at every match, since it made her feel as if she was being controlled and pressured all the time.

Tamara had obliged, but she had really missed the enjoyment of watching her daughter play. Even more, she mourned the end of the closeness they'd once shared.

Sabrina was talking and laughing with her teammates, but Tamara noticed that her head was not really in what she was saying. She kept looking around, as if her mind and spirit were elsewhere.

Tamara knew her daughter was not searching for her. As a matter of fact, Sabrina didn't even glance at the bleachers once—something she had always done in her early teens. She had always maintained that just having her mother near helped her through the tough times, when her opponent was cheating on line calls or utilizing gamesmanship, or when she was not playing particularly well that day.

It was painful to realize that maternal moral support had become so unimportant all of a sudden.

As all the girls were called to order and both teams were introduced by their respective coaches, Tamara noticed Sabrina's unnatural antsiness. It did not bode well for her match, because one aspect of Sabrina's game that could be counted on was her coolness and calmness under fire. Mentally, Sabrina had always been strong. And morally, even stronger. She always afforded her opponent the benefit of the doubt, in fact giving points away because cheating was so abhorrent to her.

As soon as the girls from both schools were matched up and began warming up on the newly resurfaced hard courts, Tamara felt her stomach clenching.

Sabrina was not concentrating. Her opponent did not have nearly half the strokes and talent Sabrina did, but she was going to win the match.

After the coaches announced that warm-up was almost over and that the girls should finish taking their serves, Tamara noticed that Sabrina was not even following her ritual of drinking some ice water, drying her hands, and checking the tension on her racquets. She just unzipped the cover, took out a racquet without looking to see whether it was her favorite one, haphazardly dried her face, and looked around.

When Sabrina's gaze went right over her, Tamara was not sure whether her daughter was ignoring her because she had not gotten to drive the Mustang, or if she simply hadn't noticed her.

Either way, it signaled disaster.

Tamara swallowed, apprehension seizing her.

When both girls approached the net, shook hands, and decided on whose racquet to spin to determine who'd serve first, Tamara unconsciously moved forward in her seat. Sabrina won the toss, and chose to serve.

And promptly lost it.

Sabrina was down three to love in no time at all. During the changeover, Tamara hoped Sabrina would assume control of herself, and concentrate on the match.

But Sabrina's focus seemed to be on the stands. She looked about expectantly. Tamara glanced around too, but she couldn't see Christopher either.

Sabrina served, and had three aces in a row. Then she lost three consecutive points. Tamara winced. Before long, Sabrina was down one to five, and after three loose returns, it was set point.

She felt someone sit down next to her, and automatically moved over to give the late arrival room.

"How's she doing?"

Startled, Tamara looked up to see Bronson, dressed incongruously in a suit, smiling down at her.

"Not good." Even as she said the words, Sabrina netted an overhead.

"She never misses an overhead," Tamara said in an agonized tone.

"It *is* quite windy," Bronson said, the sympathy of another tennis parent lacing his voice.

Tamara couldn't help smiling, if just for a moment, recalling his critical reaction the first time he'd seen Sabrina's game. They'd come a long way in such a short time.

Tamara took her eyes off the shiny green courts long enough to appreciate how handsome Bronson looked in a gray suit, and rose shirt. He'd removed his tie and opened the first few buttons on his shirt. Fine dark hair peeked through the opening, and Tamara wondered what it would feel like to run her fingers through that hair, and feel the smooth muscle underneath.

Most of the men Tamara knew would not be caught dead in a light pink shirt, but Bronson was so quietly, self-assuredly masculine that the color served only to accentuate his tanned, striking looks.

Catching the tenor of her thoughts, Tamara reminded herself that her experience with handsome men had not been of the successful variety. She'd better slow down.

Only it was easier said than done. Being with Bronson was the same as riding a superfast, suicidal roller coaster.

Forcing her attention back on to the first court, Tamara heard Cathy Sanderson announce the score. Loudly. And why shouldn't she? She was up two to one in the second set.

"Is Christopher here?" Tamara asked.

"Yeah. He's over by the fence, to offer Sabrina some support and loud cheering. Jonathan drove him over."

"Oh, I thought you'd brought him."

"No. I can't stay long. I just came to see you—but I have to get back to work soon."

Tamara smiled up at Bronson, grateful for his presence. Her incipient ulcer might not feel any better, but he could help distract her from the clinic of errors Sabrina was displaying.

Sabrina had apparently noticed Christopher too, because all of a sudden she raised her game to another level. She hit two aces and a service winner in a row. And when a strong second serve elicited a weak return, Sabrina put it away with a crisp volley winner.

"I can't believe Sabrina's down to that girl," Bronson said, shaking his head.

Tamara nodded grimly. "They've met five times before—three times in high-school play, twice in the juniors—and Cathy never even managed to get a set off her."

"She's coming back, though. It's three to two, now," Bronson said as the two girls changed sides.

Tamara noticed Christopher running around the outdoor courts, which were split in half—six courts on each side.

"She's going to lose," Tamara told Bronson.

"Kind of negative, aren't you, Mom?" Bronson said jokingly. But she noticed a gentle note of rebuke in his tone.

"Believe me, Bronson, I wish I weren't so sure of the outcome. But I know Brina. I've watched her play since she was six. I never pushed her onto matches too early, like other parents I know, who had six- and seven-year-olds, scared and crying and barely able to count, playing in the tens-and-under. I've always tried to give Sabrina a normal life. But I know her game. And she's going to lose this one. Cathy is a fighter, and she won't let go. She smells blood."

Bronson put a comforting arm about her shoulders. Tamara leaned into him for a moment, savoring the closeness and support.

Sabrina put some feeling into the match, and managed to get it into a tiebreaker—which she promptly lost seven to three.

Gracious to the end, Sabrina wiped her hand on her skirt, shook her opponent's hand, and congratulated her.

Although her teammates gave Sabrina pats on the rear and told her the usual—"Good Match!" and "You'll get her next time"—even Sabrina in her self-absorption noticed that the support was lukewarm.

Her glance swept the bleachers and found Tamara. She started smiling, but when she saw Bronson's arm about her mother, Sabrina frowned and turned away.

Bronson removed his hand from Tamara's shoulders. "Did I mess up?" he asked guiltily.

"Sabrina is the last one who should throw stones. Her behavior today was inexcusable."

"You're not going to give her a hard time because she lost, are you?"

Tamara laughed. "I'm a sports psychologist, Bronson. I know all about pressure. And I also know about not giving your best. Being preoccupied with a boyfriend is no excuse for letting down your school and other team members."

"Would you be so furious if there wasn't the danger that the kids'll get married?" Bronson asked quietly.

Tamara answered slowly, "I don't know." She sighed. "I find it hard to accept the fact that she's throwing both her education *and* her future in tennis away—after all the sacrifices, hard work, and years perfecting her craft."

"Everyone deserves the right to change their mind."

"I guess you're right," Tamara said reluctantly.

"Hey, how about the four of us catching a bite to eat before I get back to work? I'll have to spend the night there...our deadline is tomorrow."

"Poor baby," Tamara said, raising her hand and stroking Bronson's stubbly cheek in commiseration. He turned his head and deposited a kiss on her palm. It could have been an innocent gesture—but it wasn't.

Tamara removed her hand quickly, narrowing her eyes against Bronson's gleaming, laughing gaze.

But not before he noticed the shiver that perceptibly shook her frame and brought added color to her wind-rosied cheeks.

Thirteen

"**W**hat do you mean, you've been offered a football scholarship?"

"Well, you know, Dad, I've played football before—"

"Yes, just as you've played soccer and basketball and baseball—you've been cross-training. Boys take longer than girls to develop in tennis, but now's the time for you to specialize. That's what you've been doing the past two years."

Tamara saw the look that passed between Christopher and Sabrina, and thought, *Uh-oh, here it comes.*

The four of them were sitting at a new pancake house that had opened during World Cup fever, had made a name for itself during the Taste of Chicago, and was now one of the hottest places around.

Neither Sabrina nor Christopher had patronized the Palacio Internacional de Panqueques before, and had therefore been amenable to bribery.

Before dropping his little bombshell, Christopher had put away amazing amounts of German, Swedish, American and

South American pancakes, and Sabrina had not been far behind. She'd even indulged in coffee—a great weakness of hers—which she normally did not do.

Although, Tamara thought with residual bitterness, there were a lot of things Sabrina was doing that she had refrained from before.

"Like I was saying, Dad, you've been so busy, with work and all, and not always around—"

Bronson had apparently seen the light, and it was the proverbial runaway locomotive.

"Are you telling me you've been playing basketball and soccer and football behind my back? You couldn't . . . there would have been schedule conflicts—"

Christopher shook his head. "Just football, Dad. That's why we were at Notre Dame so early. I was being interviewed by two coaches—one in the morning, before my warm-up with Bree, and the other in the afternoon. That's why the tennis recruiter was so interested in getting me on his team right away—he doesn't want to lose me to the football team. He says that all the best men athletes choose football, basketball or baseball."

"Smart man. And a lucky one, who knows more about my son's schedule and future plans than I do," Bronson said with a sarcasm Tamara had not heard before.

To defuse the situation, Tamara interjected softly, "Remember what you said about the right to change one's mind?"

"But not to practically live a double life behind a parent's back," Bronson said, his eyes glittering coldly, his voice deadly low. "So not only were you planning on marrying without our knowledge, but you were going to accept a football scholarship? And when were you planning on honoring me with this revelation?"

Christopher looked at Sabrina, and back at his father. He squirmed as if he were seated on the electric chair.

"Nothing's been decided yet, Dad. There's nothing definite. But I've been recruited, and the coaches all say—"

"Does this have anything to do with Sabrina?"

"Well, my decision will certainly concern her, Dad, but I've always been interested in football. It was you who was always opposed, saying that my athletic skills were such that I should choose the sport with less chance of crippling me for life."

Bronson grabbed his coffee cup with both hands, and Tamara was afraid he'd break it and cut himself. She put her hand on his, and he looked up, divining her thougths. After gulping down the contents of his cup—Tamara was sure he wished he'd had something stronger to toss back—he pinned his son with a look that held a large measure of hurt mingled with anger.

"So I've been busting my buns all these years, putting in so many hours to give you the best, and this is how you repay my efforts."

"I knew what your answer would be, Dad. But I have to do what's right for me."

"Are you telling me you hate tennis?"

"No, of course not. I just—"

"Would you prefer to end up a cripple, with early arthritis, and God knows how many operated-on parts?"

"It doesn't have to come to that, Dad. With all the medical advances like arthroscopic surgery—"

"All the advances cannot protect you from being hit, time and time again. I take it you'd be playing quarterback?"

"Well, yes, that's my position. But I'd be protected—"

"Like *I* was in high school? You'd be able to guarantee that some behemoth on the other side didn't destroy your knee, and shoot the possibility of a college scholarship all to hell?"

The silence that enveloped the table was deafening.

"I—I didn't know, Dad. You never told me—"

Bronson picked up the check, and threw some bills on the table.

"I never saw the need to burden you with any details. But I always thought that when you told me you were somewhere—like the library, or at your group tennis lessons—you'd be there. I guess I was an idiot to take you at your word, wasn't I?"

Tamara could feel for Christopher. He'd just dropped some heavy news on his dad and was looking none too happy. But her allegiance lay with Bronson. She could palpably feel Bronson's pain and disappointment. There was nothing on this earth that hurt a parent more than a child lying, or betraying the fabric of trust.

How fragile a fabric—and how very hard to repair...

The drive home was oppressively silent. Tamara thought ahead to all the work she still had to do, and for one of the few times in her life she felt discouraged. She even indulged in feeling sorry for herself.

She not only had to deal with Sabrina's defection, but had also been faced with Bronson's pain.

What frightened Tamara was how much of that pain she'd shared with Bronson. Which showed her how deeply she was coming to care for him.

On the surface, Bronson and her ex-husband might have a lot in common. But underneath the pretty wrapping, Bronson had a depth and substance that made him into a real, fully dimensional human being.

Sabrina didn't speak until they were in the house, and Tamara was not averse to the quiet. Christopher had gone home with Jonathan, where he intended spending the night, and Bronson had not nixed the idea. He was not going to be home himself, but Tamara suspected that Bronson would not be too keen on having his son around when he *did* get home.

Something Christopher could not have failed to notice.

"You were pretty disappointed in me today, weren't you?" Sabrina asked when Tamara went into the kitchen to heat some water for tea.

Tamara looked at her daughter absently, and Sabrina repeated the question.

"I wasn't upset about your losing, if that's what you're asking."

"No, you were just unhappy about the way I lost," Sabrina mimicked her mother to perfection.

Tamara was too bruised to take new offense.

Her silence seemed to irritate Sabrina, who added, "I think that's a cop-out. I think all parents really care about is that their kids win—no matter *how* they do it. They just talk about not giving a hundred percent. But there were plenty of times when I just gave fifty percent, and still won. I didn't hear you complain about those times, and parents and coaches never do."

"Is that so?" Tamara said, stung by the unfairness of the remark. "How conveniently you forget the various coaches you've had at different stages of your career taking you to task for your poor footwork, or strategy, or lazy strokes, or poor shot selection—even if you won. Beating a weak opponent brings no glory."

"There's always more pressure in losing to someone below you."

"I'm not talking about ranking here, Sabrina, and you know it," Tamara said, leaning her hips against the kitchen sink. "Were it not for the fact that colleges place such emphasis on national rankings, I could not care less about them. I've always emphasized developing your game, and having pride in what you do. Whatever you do—"

"—deserves being done well, yak, yak, yak," Sabrina said.

Tamara realized her daughter was trying to pick a fight to avoid looking deep into herself, and she refused to oblige.

"No one's a robot," Sabrina went on. "Everyone has off days. You can't expect me to win all the time."

"What I *do* expect you to do is to have some pride, and exercise your sense of responsibility toward your school, coaches and teammates—and especially yourself, all of whom you let down today, Sabrina."

"You're just so—so inflexible," Sabrina said, cut to the quick. "I told you I had a bad day—my serve was off. And you should be more understanding."

Tamara had always been there to soothe over her daughter's losses, but she was not going to sugarcoat things again. "Your serves were off because you were looking everywhere *but* at the court. It's a testament to your talent that you were even able to *find* the service box when your eyes were so busy looking for Christopher, and exchanging heated glances when you did find him."

"Mother, it's obvious that you hate the man I love—and I hate *you!*"

Sabrina left the kitchen at a dead run, and Tamara wearily turned off the burner. She filled a teapot with hot water, knowing she was going to have a long night.

It was really lucky that she did have her work to concentrate on, because the town house—and especially the kitchen, always a safe, cozy haven—did not feel like much of a home anymore.

Tamara knew she should try to talk to Sabrina, but felt it wouldn't do much good. Her daughter was casting her mother into the role of persecutor, and herself into her latest St. Joan of Arc mode.

Sabrina's harsh words had hurt, but Tamara was not going to hold her breath waiting for an apology.

Pouring herself a steaming cup of tea, Tamara sat herself at the kitchen table to enjoy some much-needed solitude before tackling the work that awaited her.

When she heard Sabrina taking the steps three at a time, she brightened. Maybe her daughter was coming to tell her she was sorry, after all.

No such luck.

"Mother, do you mind if I go over to Kelly's house?"

"If that's where you're really going, no. But if you're planning some secret tryst with Christopher—"

"Then you wouldn't know about it," Sabrina said. "And don't worry, I realize you don't trust me as far as you can throw me, so I already told Kelly you're driving me over. You can even talk to her parents if you don't believe me."

Tamara finished her cup of tea, and decided to put the rest in a thermos. Maybe she'd drive for a little while, get the cobwebs out. Leave the house that lately seemed so empty and cold.

"Do you want some tea? Or dinner before you leave?"

"Mother! How many times do I have to remind you that unlike other people I know, I watch my caffeine intake? I'm going to eat at Kelly's house. Her mother is making a low-fat, low-cholesterol dinner for both of us, since Kelly's on a diet."

With herculean effort, Tamara refrained from reminding her virtuous daughter that she'd had three cups of regular coffee at the pancake house—plus countless pancakes topped with fat-loaded whipped cream and tons of maple syrup.

"Do you have your books, everything you need? A nightgown, toothbrush—"

Tamara heard herself and winced. She didn't have to wait long.

"I'm old enough to take care of myself, Mother. I have everything I need in my backpack. Can we just get going?"

Once a mother, always a mother, Tamara told herself ruefully.

Unfortunately, that reality would remain foreign to her daughter until *she* herself became a mother.

Tamara didn't bother to point that out, though. Like many things in life, you could repeat it until you turned blue, but only experience brought the concept screamingly to life.

After dropping Sabrina off at Kelly Masterson's house, Tamara drove for a while, listening to Pavarotti and Placido Domingo. Rather than cheering her up, the beautiful voices and poignant songs made her even sadder, and her sense of loss more profound.

Putting on her daughter's favorite station brought back memories of all the tournaments she'd taken Sabrina to, and how she'd become so used to listening to Bon Jovi, Madonna, Guns n' Roses and Bryan Adams that she'd learned the words by heart.

The good old days. Who knew they'd be over so soon?

This was tougher than she'd thought, Tamara mused as she found a talk show. The experts went on and on about how to raise children, about all the correct ways of dealing with them to allow them to reach their full potential and respect their privacy and make them productive, non-dysfunctional individuals. But everyone forgot about the parents.

And no manual could ever predict the unpredictability of a teenager, and his or her constant mood swings.

Without conscious volition, Tamara found herself driving toward Bronson's company. Figuring that since she was in the neighborhood, she might as well drop by, Tamara decided to pick up something to eat for the elder Mr. Kensington. Pizza and ice cream sounded perfect.

Parking next to Bronson's car, Tamara loaded her arms with food, drinks and dessert, and explained the situation to the security guard.

He unlocked the door for her, guided her to the section of the factory where Bronson was working, and allowed Tamara to surprise him.

Tamara noted that Bronson had changed into jeans and a T-shirt. The soft cloth of the jeans delineated his wonderful buns, and clung lovingly to his front, too. The black T-shirt enhanced every ripple of muscle, and Tamara found herself salivating for more than food.

But first things first, she told herself shamelessly.

She had to feed Bronson, to make sure he was strong enough to work all night.

Among other things.

Tamara stood there for a few seconds, drinking in the sexy sight of him, but either her presence or the delicious aroma of the pizzas—one plain cheese, one loaded with options—must have given her away, for Bronson turned suddenly.

Fourteen

Bronson stood frozen.

He couldn't believe his eyes.

After everything going wrong—the crisis with the business, the episode in Notre Dame, and now the latest bombshell from Christopher—Bronson felt as if he'd been caught in a whirlwind.

He'd always felt in total control of his life.

But he had not counted on meeting Tamara.

Of all the things that had happened lately, she was the most disconcerting. Distracting. And delicious.

The last thought reminded him that he seemed to have smelled food. And he was really starved.

But he knew what he was most hungry for.

Without talking, he closed the distance between them in three long strides, disposed of the packages, and took Tamara in his arms.

"God, am I glad you're here."

His kiss ate whatever words she'd tried to utter, and after a shocked instant, Tamara seemed neither to remember nor to care. Her hands went about him, holding and caressing, soothing and exciting, seeming to sense his need.

For his need was indeed great. He had not been celibate since his divorce, by any means, but with no relationship had he felt such a consuming desire, one that melded intense physical need with personal liking and respect.

And the way Tamara had responded to him indicated that she was attracted, too, but more important, that she had a generosity of heart that reached out to him and encompassed him in its warmth.

His lips opened hers, and his tongue played with her teeth, and when she responded in kindred abandon, he invaded her sweet, warm cavity, mirroring the action of his hips against hers.

He groaned in husky satisfaction, and he lowered his hands to her bottom, cupping it and bringing it closer to his pulsing length.

Tamara's senses swam. As he freed his mouth to trail a rosary of fiery kisses down the side of her neck, nipping at her ear in the process, and then resuming the stinging procession down the line of her throat, she pushed against him. Weakly.

Tamara realized they were moving when Bronson's mouth returned to hers and once more stole her breath and sanity away. Lost in the mists of passion, she became aware of the feel of his leg between hers.

Bronson was leading her backward, his hands whispering across her back, his invasive knee wonderfully abrasive. And then she was being lifted onto a table—a table that felt hard and cold underneath the thin slacks she was wearing.

She curved her legs about his hips and felt his manhood, strong and sure, against her belly. Desire writhed through her, and she pulled her lips away from his to taste his neck, to take sharp, tiny bites of the skin that smelled of honest work and arousal and his own incomparable, distinctive scent.

A shudder went through his body, and he pressed himself harder against her, as if wanting to be buried inside her, to be joined to her through the barriers of slacks and jeans and underwear. His mouth blindly sought hers, feverish and demanding as it savored her throat and cheeks before capturing her lips, stopping her sensual torture, and initiating one of his own.

Then, with a husky moan, he tore his mouth away, and leaned his forehead against hers.

Tamara heard his heavy, tormented breathing, and knew her lack of oxygen was also evident in the heaving of her breasts. Her nipples were pouting, and, as if sensing her need, he raised his hands from her waist to cup the engorged fullness of her breasts, and massaged them gently.

She moved her hands and put them over his, and labored to steady her breathing. After a few seconds, both regained some semblance of control, and Bronson shifted slightly to look ruefully at her.

"Sorry about that. I really lost it there for a while."

Tamara smiled, her eyes luminous, her voice husky. She was not the least bit offended. "You weren't alone. I don't think you saw me fighting you, did you?"

She dropped tiny kisses on his mouth, licking his lips, and Bronson groaned. "You are an evil woman. Please help me out here. I'm trying to be a gentleman and not take you on this very cold, unforgiving surface."

Tamara pushed gently against him and hopped down from the surface in question.

"You're right. My bottom thanks you. What we need is something more comfortable. And private. Like your office, perhaps?" Her words shocked even herself.

Bronson's face was a kaleidoscope of emotion. From surprise to incredulity to laughter to hopeful inquiry and finally undisguised hunger. "Did you come bearing gifts?"

Her husky tone stoked the fire in his eyes.

"Did I need to?"

"Hardly," he answered with gratifying quickness.

Rapidly picking up the cartons of pizza, ice cream and beverages, he put them in her arms and instructed, "My field office is down this corridor, past the loading dock, and to the right." He picked up a phone, and added, "I only have a skeleton crew at this hour. My men are burnt out from overtime, so let me get someone to cover for me here, and I'll meet you there."

Tamara nodded, but Bronson was already punching some numbers, and giving someone named Crucero instructions.

Feeling somewhat self-conscious, she followed his directions, passing some cranes, giant movable ladders, and an island full of vehicles that looked like go-carts before spying the loading dock. From there she saw an office with a sign that read BRONSON KENSINGTON in bold gold lettering against a black background.

Balancing the pizzas on her knee, she managed to pull on the knob and get the door open. A few seconds of stumbling around in the dark yielded a light switch, and as she turned it on, Tamara was pleasantly surprised.

The office was not ostentatious, but rather, like the rest of the factory, concentrated on the functional. Still, the quality of the mahogany furniture, with leather and brass features, gave an impression of quiet elegance and solidity. The most imposing items in the brown, black and gold décor were a huge desk with an equally large swivel armchair, and the couch that dominated almost a whole wall.

"I sometimes sleep at work when I have a deadline on a big order, and I know that Christopher is over at someone's house."

Startled, Tamara almost dropped the food.

Bronson came over and retrieved her purse and the packages from her, carelessly dumping them on a nearby table.

Obviously, his mind was still on something other than eating.

And as he walked slowly toward her, his feet silent on the thick carpeting, his eyes hypnotic midnight pools, she forgot the awkwardness of the moment. The stirring of their breaths were the only sounds in the office, and when Bronson took his gaze away from her for just an instant to turn on a desk lamp, lock the door and turn off the ceiling light, she felt bereft.

But not for long.

She could feel the pressure within her begin to build. She could see his tension in the ticking of a vein in his neck, and sense it in his body heat as he crossed the room slowly, inexorably.

The fire within them had ignited as a tiny spark when they'd first met, and it had smoldered as they'd tried to bank it while dealing with the difficulties that both united and divided them.

Needing to speak to end this unbearable tension, she told him in a throaty murmur, "A physical relationship is not going to make things any easier."

Bronson nodded as he drew even with her, and his hands went to her hips. "It will probably complicate them," he agreed, and Tamara heard the raw need in his voice, felt it in the way his fingers dug into her flesh. "Do you want to stop?"

Tamara thought of all the sane reasons why she should. She could still change her mind. It would be the judicious, practical thing to do.

But she found that she was tired of being sane and responsible. What she wanted, craved right now was the man right in front of her: Bronson.

And as he lowered his hands to her thighs, and then ran them up again before curling them about her derriere, she could tell that he wanted her, too.

"It would be the sensible thing to do," Tamara said even as she raised her arms and linked them about his neck. "But I'm not feeling the least bit sensible tonight."

"Good," he murmured against her mouth as his tongue swept across her upper lip, and his teeth nibbled on the full lower one.

A yearning sound escaped her, and he probed between her lips, rubbing his tongue against the roof of her mouth, and then delving deeper, stroking the inside of her mouth, swirling and searching until it mated with her tongue.

She responded by going on the attack and meeting the tip of his tongue with hers, then circling, and stabbing, dueling with him until she captured his tongue and sucked on it feverishly until he moaned inside her mouth and had to surface for air.

Bronson pushed her away, gasping, and Tamara looked at him wonderingly.

Had *he* changed his mind?

From the feel of his manhood against her stomach, she knew his yearning matched hers. Why, then, was he putting a halt to their fine madness?

"I'm . . . afraid . . . I don't have any protection," Bronson gasped. "I didn't expect the pleasure of your visit."

Tamara smiled. If anything, his concern served to heighten her already sky-high emotions.

"I do."

"So you *did* come bearing gifts, seduction in mind," Bronson said, reaching for her again.

Tamara laughed, shaking her head. "I'm afraid I was originally only going out for a drive, but that turned into a friendly dinner suggestion—"

"And an even friendlier proposition," Bronson said, looking puzzled in turn as she stayed out of range of his arms and dug into her purse.

"I'm afraid I've had these since the time you acted so shamelessly in my living room, while I was innocently trying to watch a science-fiction classic."

Tamara started to take out a condom, but Bronson snatched her purse and grabbed all of them.

"Once is not enough," he told her, turning off the desk lamp.

"But how will we be able to see—"

"When your eyes get accustomed to the darkness, you'll be able to distinguish things by the light filtering in from outside underneath the door. I want to make sure no one disturbs us—and if worst comes to worst, we'll just go by touch."

Tamara felt the displacement of air as Bronson approached her again. He moved her gently toward the couch, and she found she couldn't see a thing. But, as he'd so wisely suggested, she relied on her other senses.

In a way, the total lack of visibility was liberating. It released her from any inhibitions—not that she was feeling particularly shy at the moment. Her need was too urgent, and her desire to please Bronson too great.

Raising her hands, she found his chest and peeled the T-shirt away from his body. Bronson returned the favor, and his fingers caressed and molded even as his hands divested her of her garments.

Her own hands went on an orgy of discovery. She couldn't see the curves of his muscles, but she could feel the peaks and valleys, the dents and ridges, and when she made rough contact with his nipples, she found them already diamond-hard.

Bronson's leg insinuated itself between her thighs as he eased her downward onto the couch. The leather was a cold shock against her bare back, and Bronson quickly turned her on her side, and then positioned her above him.

"I'll warm up the sofa for you," he told her against her neck, his tongue laving her skin and his teeth taking little nibbles that sent shivers skipping along her nerve endings.

Tamara arched her back, her hands keeping her chest away from Bronson's, and his hands found her breasts, kneading the swollen globes with a gentle touch. As she raised a knee and placed it near his manhood, rubbing slightly, his kneading increased in fervor, and Bronson lifted his head to take a nipple into his mouth. One hand went to her panties, pulling them down from her taut bottom, and the other unerringly located her other breast and zeroed in on the engorged bud, circling it and fanning, until Tamara's breathing became ragged under his maddening ministrations.

Ripping the only cloth separating them, her bikini brief, down quivering thighs, Bronson nipped on the captured nipple, and then sucked it deep into his mouth.

Tamara felt as if she were disintegrating. She kicked the lace bikini away and clasped Bronson's head to her breast, not wanting the sensory onslaught to end.

Bronson's lips continued their attack on her breasts, alternating between them with a pulling, sucking frenzy that paled when his hand found the silky junction at her thighs and slipped inside.

His fingers created an unbearable friction that started a trembling through her limbs and then her entire body. His touch increased in pressure and speed, circling and dancing until she gasped for him to stop.

But rather than desist, Bronson took a throbbing, puckered nipple deep into his mouth, and then pressed his long middle finger deep into her, until she had no more control over her shivering need and closed about his hand in helpless, rippling convulsions.

When Bronson removed his mouth and hand, she almost cried out at the intense deprivation the absence of his touch aroused. But the desolation was soon cured as Bronson shifted her slightly, sheathed himself with a condom, and maneuvered her below him.

Tamara opened herself to him and he penetrated her with no preamble. She was wet and ready for him, and as he palmed her derriere, she spread wider to accommodate him.

Their stomachs convulsed reflexively against each other, and Tamara raised her legs to circle his waist as his pumping increased in depth and ferocity. Riding the pounding rhythm with Bronson, Tamara felt her senses spin in a vortex of pleasure-pain, and then the tremors were claiming him, and she buried her face into the hollow between his shoulder and throat and held on for dear life as her hips lifted to meet him and they dissolved together in a primal, consuming universe. . . .

Minutes—or was it aeons—later, they surfaced from their breathless abyss, and Bronson reached out for something in the dark. Tamara heard a muffled crash on the carpeted floor, and then a light came on. Bronson had moved the desk lamp closer to them by pulling on the chord.

The sudden illumination made her blink . . . and what she saw made her gulp with renewed longing.

His eyes were almost blue-black with desire—and with something more that took her breath away...tenderness. She had always thought the sexiest thing on this earth was to have a strong man show his softer side, reveal his vulnerability. Only the truly strong could be truly gentle.

"Are you hungry or thirsty? The ice cream is melting. I didn't mean to make you miss dinner." As his eyes roved over her still-damp body, Tamara felt she should have been self-conscious, but wasn't. Everything about being with Bronson felt right. She stretched her legs and threw her arms over her head, and noticed Bronson's gaze greedily follow the effect her catlike arching had on her body.

"We can always refreeze the ice cream. But if you're hungry, I can always take a little nap—"

"Are you kidding?" Bronson said, ripping open a condom. Tamara looked down past Bronson's wide shoulders, past his muscular chest, past his flat stomach to the manhood that was rising proudly from its dark nest.

His gaze locked with hers as he quickly put the protection in place, and then he was turning off the light again, and joining her on the sofa.

With little effort, he lifted her and sat her on his stomach. "Would you like to do the honors?" he asked as he ran his fingers up the inside of her thighs.

Tamara scratched his chest slightly, seeking and finding his nipples, and then she was leaning over him, her mouth ravenous against the wonderful saltiness of his skin.

"It'll be my pleasure."

Fifteen

"**I** love your office," Tamara told Bronson as she leaned back against him. "And this sofa is incredible."

"*You're* incredible," Bronson said, chuckling. "This is my home away from home. I have a front office for the public, but it's here I come when I have to solve some problem, or meet with some of my top men after hours."

"Since I'm not one of your men, I gather I'm a problem you have to solve?" Tamara said, lazily running her fingers up and down Bronson's jean-clad thigh, then venturing northward to caress his lean hip, flat stomach and broad chest, which was lightly sprinkled with fine, dark hair.

"Oh, you're a problem, all right. But I think I'd like to tackle you, and keep tackling you, for a long time," Bronson said, capturing her hand and dropping a kiss on it. "I've slept on this sofa many a time, but I must say, I never knew that it could prove such a mother of invention."

"I've grown rather attached to it myself," Tamara agreed, rubbing her cheek against his shoulder, and reveling in the feel and scent of the hard flesh beneath her.

"The reheated pizza and refrozen, mushy ice cream are about the best I've had," she added as Bronson hugged her more tightly against him.

Bronson's hand lazily played with strands of her hair, and he smiled with replete languor.

"I think the stimulating company might have something to do with it, don't you think? Not to say anything about the invigorating exercise."

Tamara turned slightly to look up at him and caught his satisfied smile. "I didn't know a middle-aged father of a teenage boy had it in him, Mr. Kensington. Where *do* you get your energy?"

"Hey, watch out who you call middle-aged," Bronson growled, slipping his hands inside his T-shirt, which covered Tamara to midthigh, and tickling her mercilessly.

She laughed helplessly and tried ineffectually to push his hands away, but they slowed of their own accord, and took on a more languid, suggestive pace.

"Bronson, don't," Tamara said halfheartedly, feeling her breathing quicken and the blood start to roar in her veins again. "Come on, stop it," she repeated, capturing his conniving digits and holding his hands in her lap.

"Give me one good reason why I should," Bronson said softly, leaning toward her and dropping a light kiss on her mouth.

His tenderness was almost her undoing.

"Sabrina. I have to check up on her and make sure she's at Kelly's. And I should be home, in case she tries to call me and needs something."

"She's a big girl, and it will do her some good to wonder about where *you* are for a change."

"Bronson, I'm her mother, and I just can't—"

"Yes, you can, Tamara. You *should*," Bronson said, desisting from his seductive methods.

Tamara frowned at the serious, slightly accusing note in his voice.

"Are you suggesting I should just take off and leave my child alone?" she asked, feeling the magic of the moment fade, and the old anger at Bronson's occasional high-handedness return.

"Of course not. But she's not a child anymore, Tamara. And you're going to have to let go. Eventually. The sooner you face that fact, the better it will be. For both of you."

"You're a fine one to talk, Bronson Kensington," Tamara said, practically leaping off the couch and glaring down at him. "I don't think you're handling the separation-anxiety issue too well yourself."

"But I'm not about to go and check up on Christopher, the way you're ready to. When I raced off to Notre Dame, I didn't know who Sabrina was, or what the relationship between the two kids was. Now that I know Sabrina is not a little gold digger or doped-up hussy intent on leading Christopher down the road to perdition, so to speak, we have to let up."

"You may be satisfied about Sabrina's intentions," Tamara said angrily, crossing her arms over a chest suddenly tight with a different kind of tension. "But I'm not sure about Christopher's. He might just be trying to gain a maid and typist and practice partner, while Brina loses out all around."

"And do you think your running home right now, or your constant checking up on your daughter is going to change things? You can't be with her twenty-four hours a day. Soon she'll be eighteen, and she'll be able to do whatever she wants—even if that choice is a stupid one that leads to her throwing away her future." Patting the sofa next to him, Bronson added huskily, "Let her make her own mistakes, and learn to be more selfish, Tamara. You've lived your life for Sabrina, and if she's such an ingrate she can't see it and thank you for it, then it's *her* loss. But you can't let our kids come between us. Let go, Tamara, so that you can open yourself up to other possibilities."

"Namely you?"

"I'd *prefer* it to be me. Sabrina's just interested in living and loving right now, with no thought to the future, and although both my son and your daughter are going about it the wrong way, you've got to let her fly. Because only then will you be free yourself, Tamara. You've got to unburden the Tamara that's hidden beneath the crushing weight of responsibility and self-sacrifice and devotion. And I want the free-flying, carefree, fun woman I've just held in my arms and made passionate love with."

Tamara's gaze was bruised, reflecting the pain Bronson's words had caused. She realized that part of what he was saying was true—but he should know, better than anyone, how much she loved her daughter. It was no easy task to separate. There was no stronger bond on this earth than that of mother and child . . . it was not that easily disposed of. And with Sabrina about ready to make a giant leap into an unknown chasm, how could a mother not stand by to try and break the fall? How could he ask her just to step away?

"I'd better get home," Tamara said emotionlessly, picking up the discarded clothes from the floor.

Bronson got up and crossed swiftly to her side.

"Tamara, don't shoot the messenger, please. You know what I'm saying is true. Please don't shut me out."

Tamara refused to meet his gaze. The scent of their lovemaking hovered over them like a sensual ghost, and she knew that if she let Bronson lead her back to the sofa, she'd be lost.

And she had to be strong. For her daughter's sake.

Bronson stood there, watching her get dressed, but not attempting to stop her. She guessed he was following his newfound philosophy: letting go.

When she ran a quick comb over her hair with trembling fingers, Bronson tipped her head back with an unsteady hand.

"Are you sorry? About us?"

Taking a deep breath, Tamara looked at Bronson.

"No, I'm not sorry about what just happened in this room. It wasn't just desire, or satisfying years of sexual deprivation. I realize that our lovemaking was special, but I still can't follow your advice, Bronson. It's almost as if you're asking me to choose between my child and you. And I can't make that kind of decision."

"I would never ask you to make such a decision, Tamara. I know how painful this all this. I would just like you to think over what I said. You must have guessed how I feel about you . . . you must know, after tonight, that—"

Tamara put a silencing finger on Bronson's lips.

"Please, Bronson. Let's just let it be. I have to get home. I still have a lot of work to catch up on."

She looked for her purse, and Bronson picked up the rest of the package of condoms.

As their gazes met, Bronson said, "I think I'll just keep these, if you don't mind. I'm not ready to throw in the towel, and I think we might have need of them in the future."

Tamara took the purse he was handing to her, and looked at the shiny items in Bronson's hands.

Her cheeks aflame, her thoughts confused, Tamara chose not to say anything.

For what was there to say? She had sought Bronson out, after keeping him at arm's length. They could never go back to their previous relationship, but it was hard to define what their new one was.

And she didn't feel up to trying, just now.

She walked away from Bronson, and as she reached the door, he told her, "I'll call you. We need to talk. And about a hell of a lot more than the kids."

* * *

For Tamara, the next few days were a blur of work, tennis practice and matches leading to the state tournament seeding. Added to the pressure cooker were Homecoming-related activities—some of which Brina had so thoughtfully volunteered Tamara's services for—without consulting her mother first. Tamara found herself wishing she could grow a clone of herself.

She had held firm about not letting Sabrina have the car until the actual decorating for the game and dance. Brandy Cavanaugh had excused Sabrina from three days of practice to afford her the opportunity to participate in the fun school events that other kids took for granted.

Tamara was grateful. Even though Sabrina was the best player in the school—and in the whole sectional, having a good chance of going all the way—she'd never displayed any prima-donna tendencies. Unlike other top-seeded, junior tournament players who felt they merited special treatment, Sabrina—until her involvement with Christopher— had faithfully attended every practice session unless genuinely ill or injured. Since Sabrina hated to practice, and loved the actual playing of matches, it had been one of her more admirable traits.

Tamara was happy Sabrina had the opportunity to participate in most of the Homecoming festivities like decorating for the dance. High school life... the fun, the friendships, the carefree times... only came around once, was too soon gone, and should always be remembered as wonderful, halcyon days.

Tamara had been surprised when Sabrina had asked her to help her choose her dress. But she'd gladly left work for a couple of hours and gone to the mall, aglow with the anticipation of spending some rare, precious time with her daughter.

After a long, excruciatingly vacillating hour spent fetching and running between racks and dressing room, Tamara had sighed with audible relief when Sabrina had finally settled on a gold-and-green gown with matching gold shoes and gold clutch.

Sabrina had never been one for fancy formals, but she looked breathtaking in her dress. And also quite grown-up. Sabrina had noticed the mistiness in her mother's eyes and had said imperiously, "Mother, you'd better not get maudlin here, or I'll never ask you to help me choose anything else in my entire life."

Tamara smiled through her tears, ignoring the melodramatic threat, and, despite her daughter's pained, protesting looks, she'd hugged her hard.

"You look lovely, Brina," she told her daughter.

Sabrina took the compliment less than graciously, but stopped glowering. Apparently to make up for her surliness and impatience, she asked Tamara, "Want to go for coffee and a cinnamon bun? We haven't done that in a while."

Tamara looked at her watch. She'd promised Shelley she'd be back by two, and it was almost that now. But there was no way she was going to miss spending some time with Sabrina.

"If you're too busy, Mother—" Sabrina began in an indifferent tone, but Tamara could detect the note of censure underneath her daughter's nonchalance.

"Just checking the time. Shelley can hold the fort for a while longer. I'd love a cinnamon bun, and a cup of coffee would really hit the spot right about now."

As they made their way upstairs to the food court, Tamara saw other mothers accompanying their daughters on a shopping spree. She hated to become melancholic, but she had a hard time reconciling herself to the fact that this would be one of the last times she would enjoy such outings with Sabrina.

In the very near future, Sabrina would move more into the realm of friend than child.

And damn it, Tamara wanted to be strong and mature about it, but the empty-nest syndrome was hitting her hard....

Trying to take her mind off her sentimental thoughts, which brought to mind Bronson and his gentle, if painful, advice, Tamara asked Sabrina, "How is Meghan doing these days?"

Sabrina frowned. "How should I know? I told you we're history."

Tamara waited until Sabrina had ordered her cinnamon bun with extra cream topping and then said, "Don't you think you're being a bit harsh on her?"

"Mother, can we just drop it?" Sabrina asked, rolling her eyes in her customary alarming manner. Tamara wondered if she'd ever had that knack, but she suspected today's teenagers had developed the art to perfection. How they managed to keep their eyeballs in place and eyesight intact was a mystery to Tamara.

"No, I don't think so," Tamara said, collecting her order and then paying.

Sabrina stalked away, and Tamara thought her daughter was doing one of her offended disappearing acts. But Sabrina had obviously noticed a table being vacated, and with her characteristic quickness, had beaten three other teens to it. Great eye her daughter had, even in the midst of another episode of mother-induced emotional distress.

Sabrina's coup earned her a few nasty-sounding comments from the displaced teenagers, and Tamara was glad that she'd been too far away to hear the exact content of those edifying, descriptive phrases.

With a smug smile, Sabrina spread her bounty on the table. Tamara shook her head, wondering anew how teenagers made it through these tortuous years, seesawing from childhood to attempted adulthood from one minute to the next.

Although, come to think of it, Bronson was far removed from teenhood, and *he* had not acted like a grown-up the first time they'd met. Once again, she had to forcibly push thoughts of Bronson away. He had been invading her waking *and* sleeping moments with distressing regularity. He'd called her a few times, but she'd missed his calls, and she couldn't bring herself to return them. She still didn't know what she would say to him. Tamara's emotions bounced around like a Ping-Pong ball, alternating between anxiety about her daughter and vexing perplexity about Bronson.

Sabrina watched her mother warily, obviously expecting a reproach for her lack of manners.

Tamara smiled, and said, "Thank you for getting this table for us. I know you wanted me to be able to get back to work as soon as possible."

Sabrina blinked and stopped in midchew. Then her healthy teeth began to vigorously chomp again on the sticky, sweet concoction, and she nodded. "You're welcome."

"So, will you be double-dating with Meghan as you'd originally planned?"

Sabrina narrowed her eyes. "I just *told* you, Mother, she and I have nothing to do with each other anymore."

"I'm sure that's not at Meghan's insistence," Tamara said calmly after swallowing a bite of the delicious treat.

"Of course not. She betrayed *me*. I don't want anything to do with her."

"Are you finding it hard to apologize?"

"*Me? Apologize?* Why should I? If Meghan had cared about me, she would have kept her mouth shut. As it is, she made a mess of things."

"That's not true, Sabrina, and you know it," a voice behind Sabrina said. "You're being unfair, and you should know me better than that. I was only trying to help."

Sabrina choked on a mouthful of sticky bun, and turned around in her chair with a squeal of metal legs.

Looking from Meghan to her mother with slitted eyes, Sabrina asked, "Did you arrange this meeting, Mother? If you did, it was a waste of time."

Meghan set her own tray—filled with burritos, tacos and nachos with cheese—down on the table, and grabbed another chair. The grating sound of metal once again set Tamara's teeth on edge.

Without asking permission to sit down, the normally mild-mannered, well-mannered Meghan said, "How dare you accuse your mother? Life doesn't revolve around you, Bree…you've really become egotistical and self-centered."

That was a sentiment with which Tamara heartily agreed, but seeing that Sabrina was ready to debate Meghan on her dissection of her character, Tamara decided it was time for her to go.

At least Sabrina had not gotten up from the table in a huff.

Although she had not arranged the meeting, it seemed quite propitious. And no doubt would prove beneficial.

Without bothering to interrupt the dueling girls with anything so banal as a goodbye, Tamara grabbed her tray and quietly left.

Tamara turned around just before she left the dining area to see another encouraging sign—Sabrina stealing one of Meghan's burritos.

Looking at her watch, she noticed it was almost three o'clock. She'd better hurry if she wanted to get back to work by four.

Sixteen

Bronson found the days before the Homecoming dance to be some of the most trying in his life.

Not only was Christopher surly and uncommunicative, but he either was out of the house, or, when he deigned to stay in, remained locked in his room—no doubt conversing with the fair Sabrina.

Bronson had a bad taste in his mouth, a bad feeling in his gut.

He'd had it before the big game that had cost him his football scholarship and a chance at the type of school he had envisioned attending.

He couldn't stop thinking of the guys he knew who *had* made it to college ball—and were now either crippled or living in constant pain.

Christopher should not have to go through that—and until Sabrina stormed into his life, his son had not given it much thought. Or so Bronson had believed.

Frustrated, Bronson slammed the pot in which he was cooking Christopher's favorite spaghetti sauce, and swore.

How could he know with any kind of certainty? Bronson seemed to have lost a hold on many things in his life—the most important of which was his own child. Here he'd thought he was doing all right being both mother and father to his son, but Christopher had turned into a stranger.

Bronson realized his son was growing older, more independent—and that was the way it should be. He neither expected it nor wanted it any other way.

But he *had* expected the close relationship of father and son to continue, untainted by lies, evasions, half-truths.

Even if Sabrina turned out to be the love of Christopher's life, did his son have to turn on his own father, and betray the affection and trust they had shared for so long?

Complicating matters was the fact that although Bronson resented Sabrina's presence in his son's life, he could not in all honesty say he disliked the pretty, vivacious girl who so obviously adored Christopher.

And as for the mother... Talk about your mixed-up, screwed-up modern relationships!

Tamara had warned him that making love would only complicate things further, but Bronson had not been able to resist.

He wasn't sure what exactly Tamara's feelings were for him, or how deeply they ran. He wasn't sure even *she* knew at this stage—not with the constant worrying about her daughter. He'd left her several messages, and she hadn't returned them. Did this mean she was still mad at him?

All he knew was that he could not envision a future without her. The past few days away from her had shown him that. Life without Tamara would be a mere gray existence.

Yet, Christopher's future stood in the balance.

Tamara had told him he was forcing her to decide between her daughter and himself. He had denied it, but knew there was truth to her statement.

They were in opposite camps. If push came to shove, would he be able to choose between Tamara and his son?

Tamara thought she'd felt a certain increase in the tension between Sabrina and herself, but attributed it to the fact that her daughter was under so much pressure from the academic and athletic, not to mention the very vital, all-consuming social, fronts.

With state coming up, Sabrina was watching her diet and practicing even more intensely.

At least, that was what she'd been telling her mother.

Tamara suspected that now that the ban on the Mustang had been lifted, Sabrina was sneaking in some clandestine visits with Christopher.

But, since Sabrina was going to be eighteen soon—as both her daughter and Bronson were so fond of pointing out—there really wasn't much Tamara could do. She'd lectured and talked and pleaded—the threats had stopped some time ago—until she was blue in the face.

But that feeling of uneasiness, and impending doom was floating in the air like the cloud cover before an electrical storm.

Tamara's disturbing thoughts were interrupted by Sabrina's clarion call.

"Hey, Mom, are you still going to that sports-science conference this weekend?"

Tamara lifted her tired eyes from the special diet-and-exercise program she was devising for a new client, and looked at Sabrina.

Ready to go out and finish the last of the decorating, Sabrina was dressed in jeans and her school sweater in deference to the cooling weather. Indian summer had come and gone in what seemed a flash, and the true midwestern weather was showing its nasty muscle.

"I hadn't really thought about it. I haven't canceled the reservations, but it seems pointless now, since you won't be dateless for Homecoming, as you'd feared."

Sabrina bounced into the living room and dropped into the chair facing the couch where Tamara was sitting.

Tamara had selected dark colors for the fabric of the furnishings, and had had reason to be glad of her choice over the years. She was reminded of her foresight once again upon seeing Sabrina's sneakers brush against the sides of the chairs. With Sabrina's penchant for accidents—she was always rushing, always having a place to go, people to see, things to do—her original choice, a soft pearl gray hue, would have resulted in a stained nightmare.

"I thought you were supposed to go to all of these conventions or get-togethers, or whatever. Isn't it good for the business, contacts, that sort of thing?"

Tamara pinched the bridge of her nose and rubbed her burning eyes.

"Yes, I suppose so," she answered absently. "Although I have a lot of experience in the sports-science field—from nutrition to physical training to psychology—competition is growing. I guess it'd be nice to have the luxury of attending, but I have far too much work to catch up on."

"Maybe if you go and get more business, you could hire another person to help out. Then you wouldn't be so exhausted, and might increase business even more."

"I thought you said you hated business," Tamara said, smiling. "But that was a very astute observation you just made."

"Then you'll go?" Sabrina asked excitedly. "I mean, I wouldn't want you to miss out on it just because I have a date for the dance. I mean, if you really want me to go with you, I can cancel. I can always tell Chris—"

"That your wicked mother has tried to make your life even more miserable than usual?" Tamara asked wryly.

When Sabrina colored and looked at the tip of her tennis shoes, Tamara said, "Don't worry, Brina. I'm not going to commit suicide because you're deserting me. But I do thank you for offering to perform such a supreme sacrifice."

Sabrina looked at her short, neat nails, searching for nonexistent chips in the clear polish. It was a ploy of her daughter's that signified she was either lying or had been caught at something.

Not wanting to sound jealous—which she really wasn't—or unduly disappointed, Tamara said, "Come on, Sabrina. I'm not upset. I'm really glad you'll be going to the dance."

"Just not happy that I'm going with Christopher," Sabrina said challengingly.

"I can't deny that I wish yours were a more casual relationship," Tamara said. "Nor that he wasn't as selfish as he is, worrying about his future more than yours."

"You're wrong, Mom," Sabrina said, jumping to her feet. "Christopher cares about me above all else, and despite anything you say or do, you can't keep us apart."

"I realize that, Sabrina," Tamara said quietly. "You'll do what you want when you turn eighteen—we've already established that."

Sabrina glared mutinously at Tamara, about ready to say something, but then trotted to the hall closet to get her school jacket. She called out before slamming the door, "I'm going decorating."

Sighing, Tamara stared sightlessly at the front door for a few minutes, before shaking herself out of her painful trance and coming to a decision.

"Thanks for inviting me," Bronson told Tamara the following afternoon as they stood in the lobby of the hotel in Indianapolis waiting to check in. "I know we did not part on the friendliest of terms, and when you didn't return my calls, I figured you were still upset."

"Thank you for accepting," Tamara said, suddenly pushed into his arms as another conference attendee tried to negotiate passage through the crowded line with a large suitcase, a smaller case and a briefcase draped over his thin body. "As you said, we need to talk...and not just about the children. This event should give us more of a neutral ground to hash things out."

"Well, now that I have you in my arms—where you really belong—I'm not about to let go any time soon."

"Bronson! There are plenty of associates here and potential clients that I need to impress—and not as a sex-starved space cadet."

"Your wish is my command, Madam," Bronson said, dropping his arms and stepping away from her about an inch. "I will attempt to be as circumspect as possible, considering the persistent aching your presence always induces in me."

Color flooded into Tamara's face, and she cursed Bronson silently. Just how on earth was she supposed to concentrate on the business at hand for the next few days if her mind was bombarded by Bronson's virile image and memories of his provocative words and actions?

Surreptitiously looking about her to make sure no one had heard him, she told him in a fierce whisper, "Bronson! Don't make me sorry I invited you—"

"Discreet is my middle name," Bronson said, moving another inch from her.

Looking about him, he added, "Now *this* is what I call insightful planning," Bronson told her. "Close quarters, a beautiful woman in my arms, romantic surroundings..."

Tamara couldn't help laughing. "You are incorrigible. But remember...I'll hold you to your promise to behave."

"Well, I didn't exactly promise to behave," Bronson reminded her, his eyes alight with mischief and passion. "I just said I'd be discreet."

Tamara shook her head as they moved up the line a few feet. "Only you could find something romantic in this setup. I've gone to enough seminars and conferences to know that romance is the last thing in the planners' minds."

"I'll make up for their oversight," he promised with an outrageous wink.

This was a side of the hardworking, intense Bronson that she hadn't gotten to see yet, and Tamara found she liked it. A lot.

All of a sudden, she was glad she had invited him to come along. They really *did* need to talk, but she was sure that between their discussions and the business she would be conducting, they could squeeze in some time to do more than talk. Bronson's hot gaze was guaranteeing it.

Taking advantage of a commotion at the front desk regarding a reservations snafu, Bronson dropped a quick kiss on Tamara's nose.

"Am I to assume that we'll be saving on accommodations?"

"*I'll* certainly be saving. I can deduct this as a business expense."

"You mean I have to pay for this weekend affair? I didn't bring any credit cards or cash."

"Oh, don't worry," Tamara said teasingly. "I have enough left on my charge cards to pay for your room, too."

Bronson's eyes glinted dangerously. "Maybe I can change your mind about such frivolous spending."

"You just might," Tamara said, laughing. "Your son is really frugal, so it must be in the genes."

Tamara took off her high heels as soon as the door closed behind her, enclosing Bronson and her in cocooned luxury. Normally, the drive down from Chicago would have been an enjoyable one for Tamara, but she was exhausted.

Rather than take the short flight, Tamara and Bronson had met at her consulting business, and then driven their respective cars together. Not only did they save time by not having to fight the rush-hour traffic to O'Hare, then wait for the inevitable delays at both airports, but this way they would both have transportation, and Bronson could leave after lunch tomorrow to get back to his factory.

Bronson shrugged out of his jacket, helped Tamara with her coat, threw both garments on a nearby chair, and took her in his arms.

Cradling her cheeks with gentle hands, he looked down into eyes that were glazed with fatigue.

"Would you like to talk now?" he asked softly.

"Talking is the furthest thing from my mind at this moment," she whispered, placing her hands against his crisp white shirt and reveling in the warm strength beneath.

"I'm glad that for once we are in complete agreement."

His mouth closed the distance between them with thought-stopping languor.

Seventeen

Bronson's hands moved slowly, traveling upward and leaving in their wake a warm, delicious lassitude that spread and spread in concentric circles of desire. His fingers stroked and caressed, and when they buried themselves in her hair and cupped her head, Tamara let out the breath of longing she'd been holding, it seemed, all her life.

His lips touched hers after what seemed an eternity of wanting, satin-smooth and cool, and when his tongue probed her mouth, she joined in the ancient duel. She felt as if she were soaring, flying out of this world, and yet anchored by the very real, tantalizing presence of Bronson.

His hands spread through her hair, and he cupped the back of her head to bring her even closer. Her legs were entwined with his, and her breasts were crushed against his chest, and Tamara wanted to never let go.

Her eyes, which had drifted closed as she lost herself in the weightless world of sensation, snapped open.

* * *

Bronson sensed her change in mood before he felt the slight stiffening of her body, and he forced himself to release her.

Tamara was having second thoughts, as well they both should be. He had learned to read her in the short time they'd known each other, and he knew that she was setting aside some major internal conflicts and objections by having invited him along, let alone allowing him to make love to her again. They were both being swept away by their emotions, even as the reasoning parts of their brains were sounding a major alarm.

Bronson found that the thought of being as carried away as his teenage son was exciting ... buf scary. Actually, in his own case, his feelings were even more alarming because they were not ephemeral or an infatuation, but the very real, heady attraction between a man and a woman.

A woman who was the mother of the girl who his son planned to marry...

"Having second thoughts?" Bronson asked huskily as he lowered his hands to her waist and lightly cupped her hips.

Tamara played with the buttons on his shirt before lifting her gaze to his. What she saw there made it difficult for her to remember anything—even her apprehension at getting in so deep, so fast....

"I had them *before* asking you to come away with me this weekend," she murmured. "It's true that I'd hoped we could get our heads together to try to find a solution to the dilemma facing us."

Bronson cupped a cheek with his hand and caressed the soft skin with a butterfly touch.

"That solution will have to come from the kids—we can't let them stand between us. We have a responsibility to ourselves and our happiness, independent from theirs."

"I know that part of what you said was true," Tamara admitted, stopping the fidgety movement of her fingers and letting her hands rest against Bronson's rock-solid chest, loving the steady beat of his heart under her touch. "I realize I've been sublimating, putting all my energies into my work and raising my child. But I so wanted Brina to avoid the pitfalls—" Shaking her head in frustration, she thumped on Bronson's chest. "Why can't children—in this case young adults—be more considerate of their elders? We deserve some TLC too."

Bronson laughed, a throaty, full-bodied sound that reverberated against her closed fist.

"That'll be the day, when children consider their parents' feelings, especially after a hard day's work that includes rush-hour traffic, hours spent dodging rude or drunk drivers, and then putting in countless hours at the grind before repeating the process . . . only to be greeted by a grunt, hit for money, criticized for not understanding and interfering in their lives—"

Tamara smiled at the universal description of the martyred parenthood of teenagers, and lifted her hand to touch Bronson's lips lingeringly, before sliding it into his thick mane of dark hair.

"Are we feeling sorry for ourselves?"

"Probably," Bronson said with a smile. "Although we have more reason than most, I suppose, to be confused and rattled about our particular situation. Matrimony in its many phases and variations *can* be a mixed-up affair—especially in our case, when the parents are just as involved, if not more, than their youngsters."

"I guess maybe we should come up with a manual for teenage etiquette and consideration, but right now, I'm tempted to forget all about our mutual problems and the decision Sabrina and Christopher end up making."

"I second that motion," Bronson said, opening her dove gray jacket, and pulling the pearl gray silk blouse out of the restraint of her straight gray skirt. "I remember your mentioning our putting our heads together. From what my feeble mind can remember from that abbreviated night of passion, we also put other things together quite well."

Tamara began working at Bronson's tie, a black-and-red affair that perfectly matched the dark suit he was wearing.

"You mean the part about heating the pizza in your so-convenient microwave, and freezing the ice cream in your cute little fridge?"

Bronson started opening the tiny pearl buttons on Tamara's blouse, and scolded, "No, that's *not* what I meant. I'm referring to the fact that we did a great job of putting other parts of our anatomy together."

"But I thought you said it was an 'abbeviated' night of lovemaking," Tamara reminded him as she began undoing the buttons in his shirt with ever-increasing speed.

Bronson's fingers matched her growing velocity, and he grumbled, "Woman, you're driving me crazy. I told you once was not enough."

"But it was more than once," Tamara pointed out, her eyebrows arching innocently. "As I recall, it was—"

"Not enough," Bronson growled an instant before his mouth swooped down on hers with rapacious demand.

Tamara was more than ready to meet that demand, for she felt a ravenous need of her own. The need was more than physical: it was emotional, psychological, mental, encompassing her whole being, a being that clamored to be Tamara Hayward the woman for a while, as opposed to the mother and employer and contributing member of the community.

And she knew Bronson was the only man who could fulfill her in every way.

As the decision was made, their bodies took over. Bronson began divesting Tamara of the rest of her suit, and she returned the favor with alacrity.

In seconds, they were unclothed, their naked bodies straining toward each other.

Without conscious thought, they gravitated toward the bed, and Bronson leaned Tamara backward, keeping his weight off with one arm so as not to crush her.

As his weight settled against her, Tamara sighed with feline satisfaction.

He was right, once was not enough. Or two times, or three...

Her hands began a slow exploration of Bronson's back and buttocks, and she felt him tremble beneath her touch. His lips nuzzled her neck, his tongue did wicked things to her ear, and then he was rolling them sideways so he could have full access to her body.

His lips nibbled a line up her throat, over her chin and to her full lips, which he tasted briefly before changing directions and making her breasts the target of his insatiable mouth.

Tamara felt her heart flutter and then launch into full gallop as his hand cupped the fullness of one breast, while his mouth devoured the other one.

Her legs moved restlessly on the bed, and she reveled in the feel of corded muscle beneath the sprinkling of soft hair that maximized sensation. She maneuvered to reach his chest and drop kisses on it, and then, taking a side detour, she licked at one male nipple that shied from the contact in shock, before tightening against her touch.

"How did I manage to survive the past few days?" Bronson asked wonderingly, his breath hard and fast as he looked into her face.

Tamara saw his cheeks were flushed, and knew that she, too, was wearing the badge of heady arousal.

"Careful planning, wonderful maturity, a greatly developed sense of responsibility?"

"More like your ignoring the messages I left at work and at home," Bronson reminded her as he extracted punishment by taking a nipple between his teeth and biting lightly.

Tamara sucked in her breath involuntarily as she felt the tug deep in her womb.

"And to hell with responsibility and planning, at least for tonight," Bronson rasped against her breast, effectively stopping any further rational thought.

Tamara was lost to his touch as his caresses became more and more demanding, seemingly everywhere at once, culminating as he sought entrance to the warm and wet place between her thighs.

When Bronson's lips first touched her, Tamara bucked on the bed at the contact. Bronson kept her anchored so he could taste her more fully, and then his tongue was invading her, and his hands were keeping her prisoner while she writhed in need, trying to get away yet wanting to get ever closer, until the slight trembling turned into tremors and then erupted into a volcano of sensation....

Tamara opened shimmering eyes and met his own misty gaze. He dropped a hard kiss on her mouth with lips that tasted of her, drugging her senses even further before moving away from her.

Raising herself on an elbow, Tamara saw Bronson go to the discarded slacks on the floor, and extract a small square.

"I brought some of my own. Just in case," Bronson said, quickly moving to her side after ripping open the tiny package.

Tamara welcomed him into her embrace, and she felt him hard against her. He kissed her inner thighs before parting her legs and she luxuriated as Bronson entered by slow degrees, savoring every soft inch of femininity that sheathed him. When he stroked hard, withdrew, pumped, and then withdrew again only to return with even more vigor, Tamara wrapped her legs about him, crossing her heels behind him, and took him to the very center of her.

His breathing ragged, his voice husky as he whispered endearments, Bronson upped the tempo until everything seemed to whirl, and what little hold Tamara had had on reality vanished.

As his hands caressed her, Tamara's roamed freely over his body, and then settled on his buttocks, feeling them clench and contract under her fingers even as her internal muscles contracted around Bronson's throbbing length.

She felt him stiffen a fraction of a second before her own body convulsed, and then they were joined together in a primeval dance that eliminated the barriers of time and substance, erased the line where her body stopped and his started, so that they were made one as they cried out each other's names.

"Are you hungry?" Bronson asked an hour later as his finger made intriguing forays over Tamara's breast.

Tamara covered the roaming digit with her hand, and stopped its somnolent motion.

"Yes, I am. But that will have to wait. I still have to check in at the hospitality desk. It seems many a thing slipped my mind after we entered this room."

"I wonder why," Bronson said as he lowered his head and covered her mouth with his.

The phone rang, and Tamara moved reluctantly away.

"Hold that thought," she told Bronson as she leaned over him to reach the phone.

Bronson employed the opportunity to caress her back and derriere, and felt himself grow hard. Again.

Tamara reached behind her to try and grab Bronson's hand. It was difficult maintaining a sane conversation when her body was being aroused so very thoroughly.

"Yes, this is Tamara Hayward."

Bronson heard Tamara's breath catch in her throat as he inserted his hand between her legs, and smiled in lazy male satisfaction.

There were certainly advantages to being self-employed and having an almost-grown son, Bronson reflected, since neither his job or parental responsibilities had proved impediments to his taking off at the last minute to spend this precious time with Tamara.

"Yes, I'm glad you called. I can meet you for cocktails in an hour."

Bronson's hand stilled on her fanny in silent protest, and Tamara worked hard to keep a straight face and normal tone of voice.

"No, no, it's no imposition. I was going to go down and register for several of the seminars in any case. Just give me a chance to shower and change, and I'll meet you in the Blue Velvet Room."

"Blue Velvet Room?" Bronson asked as Tamara replaced the receiver and rested her forearms on his chest.

"The organizers of this event made up a list of three colors—blue, green and yellow—to indicate the specialty the conference members might be interested in. Yellow is for sports nutrition, green for cross-training and conditioning, and blue for sports psychology."

"Does that mean you'll be blue for the weekend?"

"Well, that means my badge will be blue. By coordinating everything—including brochures and contact lists—the event planners hope that everyone will be able to distinguish whom they want to approach just by looking at the name tags they're wearing."

"That seems awfully cold," Bronson said, raising his head to flick the tip of his tongue across her ear.

Shuddering, Tamara covered his mouth with her hand, and told him severely, "Now, stop that. I'm not only here for fun, you know. I have to meet and mingle—since I *do* want to expand the horizons of my business. I'll be adventuresome, and intermix."

She got up in one fluid movement and headed for the bathroom.

When she noticed Bronson shadowing her movements, she stopped and asked, "Do you need anything?"

"Such a loaded, dangerous question," Bronson answered, quickly reaching her side, his eyes glittering with unbanked desire.

Tamara gave him an innocent look.

"If you're hungry, you can order room service," she offered helpfully.

"I doubt room service can cater to the type of hunger I'm experiencing," Bronson said, swooping down and capturing a pink nipple in his mouth. "Did I hear mention of a shower?"

"Well, yes," Tamara wheezed as his lips closed on the hardened bud. "I was going to take one."

"Mind if I join you?" Bronson asked, moving on to the other breast, even as his hand made wonderful discoveries in the soft mound at the trembling junction of her legs.

"I suppose if we hurry—" Tamara began, raising heavy, languid arms to his shoulders to prevent herself from falling.

"No hurrying," Bronson murmured against her lips.

As they half tumbled, half walked into the bathroom and stepped under a spray of warm water, Tamara tried another weak objection. "A possible client will be waiting."

"Let him wait a few minutes. He'll be lucky to get your services—I've got first dibs at the moment. And I've been waiting for you for a lifetime, so my needs are much more urgent."

Bronson grabbed the bar of soap and began running it up and down her body, his fingers and the slippery bar combining for an intoxicating, innovative sensation. Tamara decided she was more than happy to help Bronson meet those overpowering needs.

Eighteen

The rest of the evening flew by.

After signing in and picking up her introductory folder, Tamara spent the time networking, establishing new contacts, and setting up appointments with clients.

Through the cocktail reception, Bronson remained very patient and supportive, offering helpful hints as to how to maximize her making the rounds.

He even went so far as to borrow some of her business cards. Whatever Bronson's sales pitch was, it worked wonders. She was inundated with business cards in return, from individuals or company representatives who wanted to pursue an affiliation with her.

By the time everyone congregated for the banquet, Tamara was pleasantly exhausted and delightfully on edge, knowing that after dinner and the inevitable speeches, Bronson and she would be sharing the remainder of the night.

It couldn't come soon enough for Tamara.

* * *

Bronson looked at the lovely woman sitting next to him, and felt the tendrils of desire irrevocably twisted around an even stronger emotion: love.

He was in love with Tamara, and regardless of what the two wayward youngsters decided, he was going to ask her to marry him. Their children were almost adults and would have to bear the consequences of their own actions.

But Bronson could not bear to suffer the consequences of not letting Tamara know how he felt, and of their not having a chance at a life together.

He couldn't wait to retire to their room.

Tamara and Bronson walked hand in hand to the bank of elevators. Dinner, which had consisted of steak and shrimp, a Spanish chicken dish, and a vegetarian choice, had been excellent. Some of the speeches and spiels had been long-winded, but on the whole, the affair had been a success.

She looked forward to tomorrow's full schedule, when she'd be able to attend some seminars and learn of the latest developments in the rapidly changing and ever-expanding world of sports science.

They rode the elevator to their floor with other conference attendees, so were unable to speak beyond banalities. But just being close to Bronson made Tamara feel fulfilled, happy, glad to be alive.

Bronson opened the door for them and followed her into the room.

Tamara took off her high-heeled sandals, and Bronson was immediately at her side, very helpfully reaching the zipper of her black-and-silver evening gown.

"Oh, look, there's a message for us," Tamara said, moving toward the phone.

The premonition Bronson had experienced hit him full force.

Was the other shoe about to drop?

Tamara placed a call to the front desk and listened to the clerk as he read the message to her.

Attuned to Tamara's every nuance, Bronson knew something was wrong before she turned and faced him, the receiver forgotten in her hand.

"It's from Brandy Cavanaugh. She asked that you call her as soon as possible."

His ardor cooled as if doused with a bucket of ice water, Bronson picked up the phone, his heart hammering in his throat.

He saw his own fear reflected in Tamara's eyes, and pulled her against him.

Quickly dialing his cousin's number, he spoke in a voice that was rough with worry.

"What is it, Brandy?"

Tamara swallowed as she saw the change that came over Bronson.

Whereas just a few minutes ago he'd been the attentive, affectionate lover, now the expression on his face was stormy and furious.

"Thanks, Brandy. Sorry that you have to be in the middle of all this."

Tamara breathed easier. Obviously, neither of the children had been hurt.

"Yes, I'll leave right away. And thanks again, Brandy. I owe you—not one, but several."

"Are the children all right?" Tamara asked, wondering why Bronson seemed to exude icicles as he looked at her.

"That girl of yours has really done it."

Tamara's heart beat even faster. "What happened? Is she hurt?"

"No, but she's causing irreparable harm to my son. Apparently Christopher is going to go for a football scholarship, to make it easier for Sabrina to get *her* tennis scholarship."

"And that is *my* daughter's fault?" Tamara asked incredulously, a part of her mind noting that the lovers of the last few delightful hours were once again parents first...and sadly, almost strangers.

"If Sabrina had not become involved with Christopher, he would still be pursuing a tennis career."

"And if Brina had not met *your* son, she'd never have run away or contemplated marriage at such a vulnerable age."

Bronson rubbed his hands over his face, and looked somberly at Tamara.

"Well, that doesn't seem to be in the contemplation stage any longer. As we speak, it might even be a reality."

"What are you saying? Have they actually eloped?"

Tamara stood there, trying to absorb the unsettling information. Just a short while ago, she had experienced all the fulfillment and happiness a woman dreams of. She had come to the realization—slow to dawn, but incredibly powerful when it came to full light—that she loved Bronson.

And now they were back to where they'd started from, on opposite sides of the fence. Even though they were both united in their opposition to an early marriage for their children that would most probably end in an early divorce, they were separated by their individual concerns.

Tamara was glad that her daughter would be pursuing an education foremost, and the far chancier, less likely-to-be-fulfilled goal of turning pro. But at least she was going to give it a try. That was what she'd hoped for—that Brina take a chance now so that there'd be no regrets later.

But at such a tender age, and with both Christopher and Brina carrying such heavy pressure—trying to work, not only on their marriage, but at a living, a college education, and demanding athletic goals—how would they manage?

The haunted look in Bronson's eyes tore at Tamara's heart. She knew he was experiencing a father's disappointment, but even worse, anguish about his son's physical well-being. She wondered if he could be feeling any pain over the inevitable loss of his relationship with her.

She shook the thought off. Bronson had clearly chosen his side. He was wrong to lay the blame at her door. Or at Sabrina's. Christopher was eighteen, and knew what he was doing. Brina was not forcing his son to get a football scholarship... she had only come to terms with her own future.

Bronson broke into her thoughts when he began to pack.

"I'm going after them," he said. "I've got to prevent this lunacy."

"That was my first instinct, Bronson, but it's no use. If they're already married, it's too late. And if they're not, and we manage to stop them this time, they'll only try again in the future."

Bronson stopped throwing the items in his overnight case to fix her with a cold stare.

"So you're fine with their decision?"

"No, of course not. But there's really nothing we can do. If they don't get married now, they will later. And maybe they're really in love. Maybe things will work out after all."

Bronson shook his head and resumed packing. "If their love is so strong, it will survive a separation."

"But that's hard to explain to a couple of teenagers in the throes of first love and passion," Tamara pointed out gently.

"Are you coming with me? Or is your daughter's education and tennis career more important than my son's welfare?"

Tamara paled. "That's an unfair accusation, Bronson. I know you're in pain, but *I* am too. And you're the one who taught me we have to start living for ourselves, get on with our own lives."

"Maybe *your* career is more important, then," Bronson said. "Does staying here really mean more to you than Sabrina?"

"I think you'd better leave," Tamara said softly. "*Nothing* is more important than my daughter's welfare, Bronson, but I've finally learned to let go."

Bronson fixed her with a bleak look, took his jacket, and walked to the door.

"I love you, Tamara. But I can't let this happen. My son's welfare is at stake."

Tamara's eyes stung. She watched Bronson leave, and felt as if her heart had been savaged. First Sabrina, now Bronson.

A person should not be expected to suffer two such losses at the same time.

How was she ever going to survive?

Tamara didn't know how long she stood in the middle of the room. She came back to reality when her back and legs painfully reminded her of their abused existence.

Wiping away the tears that had been silently running down her face and had soaked the bodice of her dress, Tamara got a grip on herself.

She could not fall apart. She refused to. Her daughter might need her down the line, might realize the mistake she was making.

And Tamara wanted to be as well prepared as possible—emotionally, mentally, financially—to help Sabrina out of her self-inflicted mess.

Knowing that the networking was still in full swing, Tamara changed out of her dress into a business outfit, and went downstairs to drum up business for her firm.

Bronson left the hotel torn by conflicting emotions, which continued to claw at him as he drove back to Chicago.

He was glad Tamara had suggested they each take their own car, since he'd needed to leave earlier than she. He just hadn't realized how much earlier that would turn out to be.

Although he drove over the posted speed limits all the way north on I-65, Bronson was lucky. Certain sections were known as radar alley, but the only thing on his mind was stopping Christopher from making a foolish mistake.

He felt guilt over the way he'd torn into Tamara. She had not deserved the accusations he'd flung at her in his pain and fear. After all, Tamara was going through a hell of her own right now.

But she had not seemed to understand the urgency of the situation. Christopher could end up crippled if he made the wrong career choice. The phantom of his own experience had overridden everything, including the advice he had so recently given Tamara about letting go.

He laughed bitterly as he realized he was once again racing through Indiana. He had always been fond of the state—and had admired the Irish football program as one of the best in the nation, with an excellent record for graduating its athletes. Indiana was certainly leaving an indelible impression on him.

Bronson prayed he'd get there in time.

Tamara went through the rest of the weekend in automatic mode. Although she was desperately worried about Sabrina, she forced herself to go about her business.

When Sunday morning came around, she attended an early seminar and had breakfast with a couple of colleagues.

Then she'd checked out early, skipping the afternoon functions, and gotten on I-465, the loop around the city.

She kept five miles under the limit because her brain was on overload. Being around so many people, bombarded by all kinds of new data, forcing her mind to concentrate, had afforded her some distraction.

But the nights had been lonely. And long.

Funny how just a short time ago she had felt in total control of her life.

Then she'd met Bronson and had found out about Christopher and Sabrina, and her life had not stopped spinning since.

The accusations Bronson had thrown at her had hurt. Deeply and profoundly. She understood that his pain had been great.

But what about her own worry and agony? She was no happier about the situation than Bronson was. And having found out she loved a man who loved her and seeing him walk out the door all in one day was an emotionally devastating experience.

By the time Tamara saw the sign for Purdue University about halfway home, she had come to the conclusion that Bronson could not possibly love her as he'd professed.

He must have had a fairly clear idea of what her feelings for him were—even though she had not been given the opportunity to fully express them. And still he'd left her when she'd needed him most—when they had both needed each other's support.

An hour away from home, as Tamara got onto the Skyway, she realized she was mad.

Furious.

Feeling betrayed.

The anger helped dissipate the hurt somewhat, and even better, helped her focus her mind.

She had not deserved such treatment—not from her ex-husband, not from Sabrina, and certainly not from Bronson.

And she'd be damned if she was going to take it anymore.

Nineteen

When Tamara got home, she went by her office first.

If Sabrina needed her for anything, she'd know where to reach her. Tamara had gone in to work plenty of times on Sundays for a couple of hours—and for longer periods if Sabrina was over at a friend's house for the day.

The only phone call she'd received had been from Shelley, who had the flu and would not be able to come in Monday morning.

Tamara felt like crying, but managed a laugh. When it rained...

By the time Tamara got to the town house, she almost wished she was a drinker so she could tie one on. But she'd have to settle for a long, hot bath and a bowl of chili—the hotter the better.

She'd just settled down at the kitchen table with a glass of lemon tea and the spicy chili when the front doorbell rang.

Tamara frowned. It was past ten o'clock.

Who could be calling at that hour?

* * *

Bronson looked at Tamara, who was clad in a pink terry cloth robe, her hair up in a towel turban, and felt his insides clench.

Her face was freshly scrubbed, and her normally vivid eyes shadowed.

Knowing he was responsible for putting even a portion of that pain there made Bronson want to beat himself up.

Tamara moved forward to look past him.

"Have you found them?" she asked, the hope in her voice tearing him apart.

"I haven't even looked. I just had a long chat with Brandy, and I thought I'd come over and tell you the story so far."

Tamara stepped aside, and Bronson followed her inside the house.

"Would you like some chili?" Tamara asked politely as she led Bronson into the kitchen.

"No, thank you. I'm not very hungry at the moment."

Tamara tried to eat, but found that her appetite had deserted her.

"Please, don't stop eating on my account," Bronson said as she pushed the plate aside.

"Like you, I find I'm not hungry now," Tamara said coolly. "What did your cousin say?"

"She found out from Jonathan that the kids were leaving to get married. He was feeling guilty about covering up for Christopher and called Meghan. And since you were out of town, Meghan contacted Brandy."

Tamara toyed with the condensation on the *Star Wars* glass, a relic from what she considered the good old days— a time that was uncomplicated, full of love and trust and closeness between her daughter and herself.

"Would you like some tea?" she asked.

"No, thanks," Bronson said. He sensed the tears just beneath the surface and realized what a heel he'd been, deserting Tamara when she'd needed him so—just as he'd needed her. "It seems the kids had been planning this all along, lulling us into a false sense of security."

"So all the preparations for the dance, Brina's getting a new dress and asking me to help pick it out were all a ruse?"

"Apparently Sabrina wanted to have a last memory of high school, since she'll be missing the prom. But Chris felt it'd be better if they left sooner—no one would be expecting it. So they compromised. They made an appearance at the dance. "

Tamara's laugh was bitter. "What an enterprising pair."

"According to Brandy, Meghan and Jonathan tried to stop them from leaving. But neither of our darlings would listen."

Tamara sipped at her tea silently, thoughtfully.

"Tamara, I'd like to apologize. Yet again."

"For what?" Tamara asked, shrugging. "You don't have any control over what Christopher does, any more than I have over Brina. I'm even more disappointed than before, because I told her how I felt about her lying, about her betraying our trust. And to think that she acted so buddy-buddy at the mall...I should have suspected—"

Tamara's voice broke, and Bronson said, "Please, don't. I hate to see you in pain, and it seems both of us Kensington men have given you that in spades."

Wiping her tears away, Tamara got up and briskly cleared the table. "It takes two, Bronson. Brina is just as guilty of running, and lying to me. I don't know how we'll ever go on now. I didn't approve of her getting married, but I could have accepted it in time. But this deliberate deceiving..."

Bronson stood, walked around the table, and approached Tamara tentatively, wanting to put his arms about her and offer her the comfort he'd neglected to provide earlier.

"Please forgive me, Tamara. That was incredibly cruel and stupid of me, accusing you of not caring. My only excuse—and a poor one at that, I realize—is that I was hurting. I guess both Christopher and Sabrina will have to learn their lesson the hard way."

Tamara thought things over for a minute. "Why didn't you go look for them?"

"Because of you. You reminded me that we can't chase after them and try to save them from their own actions."

Tamara leaned against the sink and crossed her arms. "Well, thank you for coming by and telling me what you've learned."

Bronson could read an off-limits sign as well as the next man, but he couldn't leave just yet. Not this way.

"You haven't really forgiven me, have you?" he asked, looking down at Tamara and realizing the space she was keeping between them was not just physical, but emotional.

"I told you, I'm not blaming you for Chris's actions."

"Just like I shouldn't have blamed you for Sabrina's," Bronson said. "Or for any decision that might have adversely affected my son."

Tamara held his gaze, but didn't let him off the hook. He had hurt her, deeply, and what was worse, had run away at a crucial time.

"But this is not what this is all about, is it, Tamara?" Bronson said, reading the accusation in her shadowed eyes.

"You're right. It goes beyond our kids, and our concern for their welfare. My ex-husband was a very handsome, personable man with a lot of friends and a bright future. But he ran—emotionally or physically—at the slightest sign of trouble."

"And you think I'm just like him—undependable and lightweight."

Tamara held his gaze. "I hadn't—until you told me you loved me, and left me in the same breath."

Bronson raised his hand and traced the soft skin of her cheek with a gentle finger.

"I do love you, Tamara. More than anything. I wasn't running away, nor was I putting my son before my feelings for you. It's just that I thought you could take care of yourself—you have, for a long time, not only of yourself, but also of your daughter. And I knew how strong you are—"

"Being strong has nothing to do with loving someone or wanting him there, Bronson," Tamara said. "I had just realized I'd loved you, too. But I was never given a chance to confess my feelings, because you just took off. Like my ex-husband did, and like your son and my daughter did. I'm tired of being deserted, Bronson. I deserve better."

Bronson dropped his hand from her face.

"I know you do." Not able to help himself, Bronson dropped a kiss on Tamara's lips, which tasted bittersweet, of lemon and a love lost. "I love you, Tamara. I had just discovered how much and planned on asking you to marry me—but I blew it. I'm sorry."

Tamara heard the pain and sorrow in Bronson's voice, but she was still lost in a whirlpool of her own hurt. She had been betrayed so often in the past—how could she trust anyone again?

Bronson studied her face as if trying to memorize her features, then abruptly turned and strode out of the kitchen.

And her life.

The desolation she experienced was profound.

The following morning Tamara woke up after very little sleep, automatically threw on a robe and slippers and padded down to the kitchen to start breakfast and get her daughter off to school.

Then she remembered that Sabrina wasn't there.

Tamara closed her eyes and leaned against the kitchen table for support, as the waves of pain invaded her and clogged her throat.

Eyes burning, Tamara refused to cry. She had done enough of that last night, restlessly tossing on a big, empty bed that should have had Bronson in it.

She had gone over his actions and their conversation a thousand times, but had always come to the same conclusion: she had been right in her original opinion of Bronson.

He was very much like her ex-husband.

Tamara didn't need a man in her life.

She had become involved with him despite her reservations regarding their conflict over their children and other issues.

And apparently she'd been right to be leery.

Thank God she had her work.

Bronson went about the factory like a robot.

He constantly cursed his stupidity at having hurt Tamara. Having abandoned her.

He'd witnessed Tamara's love for Sabrina. He knew firsthand of her courage, hard work and dedication.

He had been totally off base to blame her for anything.

And now he could not stop blaming himself.

How could he ever prove to her that he was not like her worthless ex-husband?

He, of all people, should know what desertion did to a person. He still remembered the black depths he'd sunk to after Joanna had left him and their young son. He'd thought he'd never get over it, nor be able to allow anyone else that close.

But he had. And so had Tamara.

The only problem was, Tamara had trusted him.

He cursed himself. Again.

Bronson came out of his bitter reverie when his foreman came over to ask about specifications for a certain tool, and a definite delivery date for an overseas shipment.

Throwing himself into his work, Bronson promised himself he'd find a way to prove to Tamara that he was not a deadbeat, that he was not her ex-husband, and that she'd been right in putting her trust and love in him.

He hoped it would not be too late.

Twenty

The following morning, Tamara called the athletic department and asked to speak to Brandy Cavanaugh.

She needed advice on how to handle the school situation. And she figured Christopher's cousin would have some suggestions.

Brandy's secretary transferred her right away when Tamara announced who she was, and Brandy agreed to meet Tamara for lunch.

They chose a restaurant equidistant from school and Tamara's office, since Shelley was out sick, and Tamara had to get back as quickly as possible.

Tamara spotted Brandy Cavanaugh right away.

She was a tall brunette, with wide shoulders, an athletic build, and deep blue eyes that reminded her of Bronson.

They could have passed for brother and sister.

Brandy approached her in the lobby of the restaurant with quick strides and an easy grace. Her smile was warm and welcoming.

Extending her hand, she said, "Hi, I'm Brandy. And you're unmistakably Tamara."

At Tamara's questioning look, Brandy explained, "Not only does Sabrina look like you, but Bronson has described you at length. He's even waxed poetic."

Tamara stiffened at the mention of her daughter and Bronson in the same breath. She knew Brandy had noticed her reaction, but all the other woman said was, "Do you prefer smoking or non-smoking?"

"Oh, non, by all means."

After they were seated, Tamara commented on Brandy's striking resemblance to Bronson.

"The family genes. A lot of Kensingtons have the dark hair and blue eyes."

Once they'd ordered, Brandy said, "I know I touched a raw nerve back there. Care to tell me about it?"

Tamara hesitated. "I really came here to talk about Sabrina, and how to handle her delicate situation. I'm still hoping she'll come to her senses. Can you suggest how I should account for her absences from school?" A thought occurred to her. "Unless Jonathan and Meghan already—"

"You can set your mind at ease on that score, at least," Brandy said, waiting until the waitress had set down their cheeseburgers. "I've asked both to keep quiet, hoping, as you do, that they'll return soon."

As Tamara picked at a french fry, she asked Brandy, "Do you think there's any hope of that?"

Brandy heard the forlorn note in Tamara's voice and said, "This has been really rough on you, hasn't it? Having to deal with your daughter lying to you and taking off with a boy you barely know—and then having to face Bronson's defection also."

Tamara's startled glance flew to Brandy's sympathetic one. "You know?"

Brandy smiled and took a healthy bite of her burger. She nodded, swallowed, and said, "Both Kensington men have come to me for advice from time to time. Bronson and I are very close.''

Tamara felt tears prick behind her eyelids at the understanding in Brandy's voice. ''I can't understand my daughter's thought processes lately. First she's ready to dump both tennis and college. Now she wants to pursue both a degree and tennis—yet can't see that marriage at this time is not the answer. Of course, Bronson has not been that logical, either.'' Sighing, Tamara confessed, ''None of us have.''

''And having to deal with Bronson's antiquated notions of who should be the breadwinner, and a man's education taking precedence over a woman's are not conducive to an easy, smooth romance, are they?''

Tamara smiled. ''Are you a mind reader?''

''No, I just think we're a lot alike. I'm a working woman, too, but fortunately, unlike yourself, I don't have a daughter I've raised and agonized over during the last eighteen years giving me such grief. And I know what *I'd* say if a man told me his son's future was more important than my girl's . . . and I bet my language would be a lot more colorful than yours.''

Tamara laughed, and found the next twenty minutes a pleasant break that helped take her mind off her worries. Tamara was grateful for the respite.

Her gratitude also encompassed Brandy's suggestion that Tamara call Sabrina in sick. Her grades were such that she could stand to miss a few days.

As the waitress brought their checks, Tamara insisted on paying for the meal.

''It's the least I can do,'' Tamara said. ''You've been very helpful, and I know how much you've helped Christopher in the past. I guess both Bronson and I owe you.''

Brandy hesitated, something obviously on her mind.

''I know it's none of my business,'' she said in what Tamara had learned to recognize as her characteristic blunt way. ''But you ought to give Bronson a break.''

''I'm sorry. At the moment, I don't think I can—''

"I realize you're feeling raw right now. But Bronson is crazy about you, and he really *is* dependable. He's nothing like your ex-husband."

Tamara shook her head. "You *are* nosy. And does Bronson confide everything in you?"

Brandy's smile was naughty. *"Everything."* Looking at her watch, she added, "I have to get going. We have double practice today to prepare for state, which got postponed because of the weather. I just wish someone would spring to move the tournament indoors, especially since we have a pro tourney in town now, and there are just no courts to put the kids on."

Tamara paid the check and they walked out of the restaurant together.

"I know I'm meddling, but please consider giving Bronson another chance. Normally he's a rock, but like you with Sabrina, he's been both mother and father to Chris, and he's always wanted his son to have everything he never had. I guess he overlooked your feelings because he was so sure you could handle anything that came your way."

"I *can* handle anything that comes my way," Tamara said, closing her jacket against the strong midday breeze. "There was just no need for Bronson to leave me."

Brandy told her softly, "But Bronson didn't leave you. Not like your ex. He just went *toward* someone he felt needed him more than you did."

Sticking out her hand, Brandy said, "Well, I'm sure glad we've finally met, Tamara. Even if it took these kind of circumstances. And by the way, if your daughter calls, remind her that she left me minus my number one player for the state conference." Taking her car keys out of the side pocket of her Deerbrook High warm-up suit, Brandy added, "Tell her I'm so very grateful she left me in the lurch."

"Do you think she'll call?" Tamara asked, hope lacing her voice.

"I sure hope so. For all of our sakes."

* * *

When Tamara got home that evening, she saw a light in the living room. Shaking her head, she told herself that she was really losing it. Leaving a light on all day was not something she regularly did.

Rubbing the stiffness out of her neck, Tamara took off her jacket and draped it over a chair. About ready to drop into it, she sensed someone in the room.

Her heart in her throat, Tamara turned around.

And saw Sabrina sitting on the couch, cross-legged, her eyes red and puffy, her expression uncertain.

"Where's Christopher?" Tamara asked, glancing around.

"We had a fight," Sabrina said, looking wary and uncertain. "Do you want me to leave?"

"Leave?" Tamara asked blankly. The shock of seeing her daughter had paralyzed her system. She had trouble taking anything in.

"I mean, I can understand if you don't want me around. I've been mean and hateful to you, I've lied and gone behind your back, and—"

Sabrina broke down and burst into tears.

Tamara rushed over to her daughter's side and put her arms around the sobbing girl.

"*Of course* I don't want you to leave."

"But I said I wanted to be independent. No one can be independent when they leave taking a car and clothes bought by their mother, and the bank-account savings—"

Tamara closed her eyes and hugged Sabrina tightly.

"Shh, baby, don't cry. We'll work this out."

Sabrina raised a tearstained face and asked, "How can you be so nice to me after I've been so horrid to you?"

"Hasn't it dawned on you, Sabrina, that I love you to death—that I love you more than life itself, and would do anything to keep you safe? Your happiness is all that matters to me—and that was why I was opposed to your getting married so young and abandoning school. Not because I wanted to dictate your future or control you."

"Mom, I'm so sorry."

Tamara felt tears run down her own cheeks, but this time they were tears of joy and relief.

Moving slightly away so she could look down into her daughter's face, Tamara asked, "What was the fight about?"

"Christopher was having second thoughts about taking that football scholarship. He felt he was doing it as a big favor on my behalf. When I asked him what he'd rather do, he said we should do what we'd originally discussed—having me work until he got his education and tennis career on track. I told him I wasn't willing to sacrifice *my* education and future, and that he was being awfully selfish." Grabbing a tissue from the dispenser on the coffee table, Sabrina said, "So I told him the marriage was off."

Tamara sighed in relief. "I'm glad you've decided to wait."

Sabrina blew her nose noisily and added, "I told Christopher if we were meant to be, we can still get married after we graduate from college."

Tamara got a tissue and dried Sabrina's tears away. "I'm so glad you're here. There are a lot of people who love you and were hoping you'd come back—Meghan, Jonathan, Brandy Cavanaugh."

"Ms. Cavanaugh!" Sabrina exclaimed. "She must be furious at me, with state coming up."

"Well, she *did* mention you put her in a very difficult position, depriving her of her top singles player."

"I'll call her right away and tell her I'm back. Maybe I can still get in some hitting tonight."

Sabrina jumped off the couch, then came back to hug her mother. "It is okay if I continue my lessons? You're not tired of footing the bill? Or do you want me to work—"

Tamara pulled her daughter close for another hug. She couldn't believe her baby was back, and she could not get enough reassurance. She was also going to make sure that Brina never felt pressured into anything again—or at the very least, that they communicated, so that this heartbreak would not be repeated.

"I love you, Brina. Of course I'll help you, with school and tennis. If that is what you want. You've told me repeatedly that tennis was my dream. If you still feel that way, we can forget about the scholarship, and try to find another way to pay for tuition and—"

"I love you too, Mom. And I realized, once I decided to give it up, that tennis was not the issue. I realized I really missed playing and the constant challenge of not only opponents, but of becoming better and better. I was just using it as an excuse to lash out at you, and gain some autonomy and independence. I guess I went about it the wrong way."

"Let's make sure it never happens again, Brina," Tamara said, dropping a kiss on Sabrina's head. Her daughter did not try to pull away, and although Tamara knew it was temporary, it warmed her heart that for just a little bit, Brina was suffering her mother's display of affection and need for closeness.

Tamara let go of Sabrina, and she took a couple of steps toward the stairs, and stopped, turning around. "I slept with Christopher, in case you're wondering. But you don't have to worry about my getting pregnant. I made him take precautions—and he came prepared."

Blushing furiously, Sabrina rushed out of the room.

Tamara sat there, drained and relieved and happy and sad all at once.

She was sorry that her daughter had lost her virginity, but knew that it was inevitable. It meant Sabrina was no longer a little girl, and that her daughter would be faced with more complicated issues to confront. But at least she had made love for the first time with a boy she cared for, and who loved her back.

For now, at least, she'd gotten her daughter back.

But she'd lost Bronson.

* * *

Tamara and Sabrina were finishing dinner when the doorbell rang.

"Are you expecting someone, Brina?" Tamara asked.

"No, not tonight. Meghan and I are getting together tomorrow, so she can catch me up on the assignments I've missed. I don't want to lose my valedictorian status."

Tamara gave Sabrina a quick hug, and went to see who was at the door.

When she opened it, she was speechless.

In front of her stood a furious-looking Bronson and a sheepish-looking Christopher.

"May we come in?"

Tamara nodded.

"Who is it, Mom?" Sabrina called out from the kitchen. She came out and stopped dead upon seeing Christopher.

"I'll be upstairs studying," Sabrina said, heading for the steps without so much as a hello.

"Sabrina!" Bronson called out.

Before he could speak, Tamara intervened. "Whatever you have to say, you can say to me, Bronson. I won't have you browbeating my daughter."

Bronson looked puzzled. "I don't want her to leave before Christopher apologizes to her. He's behaved abominably—which seems to run in the family."

Surprised, Tamara watched as Christopher approached Sabrina and spoke softly to her.

Sabrina looked at Christopher for a long moment, and then said, "Mom, we'll be up in my room for a while."

Tamara watched as Sabrina took the steps two at a time, and turned to face Bronson.

"When Christopher came home and told me he was not sure about playing football, I was thrilled at first. But when he explained to me how he'd expected Sabrina to give up everything for him, I realized how selfish that sounded. And how things must have looked to you."

"Well, I'm glad you realized that, Bronson," Tamara said. "They seem to have learned their lesson."

"And I've learned mine. Christopher deserves a chance to choose the sport he prefers—even if it does turn out to be football. I think he was just using Sabrina as an excuse to defy me—although I know he cares about her very much." His voice dropping an octave, he asked, "Can you ever forgive me, Tamara?"

Something in Tamara's eyes told Bronson that it was safe to approach her. "Are you still angry at me?"

"Somewhat," Tamara admitted. "But I was thinking of something Brandy said—that you were running toward your son, trying to save him from his own folly. You were not running away from me—at least not permanently."

"And I never would," Bronson said, taking her in his arms. "I love you, Tamara. With all my heart, and being and soul."

The last of Tamara's doubts vanished like snow on a warm spring day.

"And I love you, Bronson," she whispered.

Bronson hugged her to him, so hard that she was afraid he'd break her rib cage. He dropped kisses on her neck, her cheek, her chin, her nose, and finally swooped down to claim her mouth.

"Ah, excuse me?"

Tamara surfaced and realized that the loud, piping voice belonged to Sabrina, and that it was coming from the direction of the stairs.

She turned in the circle of Bronson's arms and faced two smiling teenage faces.

"Yes?"

"Does that mean we'll be having a wedding after all?" Sabrina asked.

"Do either of you mind? Not too long ago you were opposed to us having anything to do with each other. I believe the term used was 'incest,'" Tamara said.

"Oh, we're grown up now," Sabrina said airily. Tamara could feel the chuckles emanating from Bronson's chest reverberating against her back. "Much more aware."

"You two going to stick it out in school, and each of you pursue your own interests?" Bronson asked.

Both Christopher and Sabrina nodded.

"It's like you said, Dad," Christopher said. "Sabrina has just as much right to go to college and try to turn pro as I do. I'm not sure yet about playing football. I was thinking of trying it out freshman year. We'll wait on the wedding. If we both dorm at Notre Dame, we can still be near each other, yet have the freedom and time to pursue our individual goals and get our college degrees."

"We're going to keep on dating," Sabrina said, looking to Christopher for confirmation. "And we'll hit with each other to keep our games sharp. But we want things to cool off for a bit. And we want to make sure we get those scholarships."

"We can count on you two to be maid of honor and best man at our wedding?" Tamara asked.

"Sure! When's the wedding going to take place?" Sabrina asked.

"As soon as possible," Bronson answered, dropping a kiss on Tamara's golden head.

* * * * *

COMING NEXT MONTH

#943 THE WILDE BUNCH—Barbara Boswell

August's *Man of the Month,* rancher Mac Wilde, needed a woman to help raise his four kids. So he took Kara Kirby as his wife in name only....

#944 COWBOYS DON'T QUIT—Anne McAllister

Code of the West

Sexy cowboy Luke Tanner was trying to escape his past, and Jillian Crane was the only woman who could help him. Unfortunately, she also happened to be the woman he was running from....

#945 HEART OF THE HUNTER—BJ James

Men of the Black Watch

Fifteen years ago, Jeb Tanner had mysteriously disappeared from Nicole Callison's life. Now the irresistible man had somehow found her, but how could Nicole be sure his motives for returning were honorable?

#946 MAN OVERBOARD—Karen Leabo

Private investigator Harrison Powell knew beautiful Paige Stovall was hiding something. But it was too late—she had already pushed him overboard...with desire!

#947 THE RANCHER AND THE REDHEAD—Susannah Davis

The only way Sam Preston could keep custody of his baby cousin was to marry. So he hoodwinked Roni Daniels into becoming his wife!

#948 TEXAS TEMPTATION—Barbara McCauley

Hearts of Stone

Jared Stone was everything Annie Bailey had ever wanted in a man, but he was the one man she could *never* have. Would she risk the temptation of loving him when everything she cared about was at stake?

MILLION DOLLAR SWEEPSTAKES (III)

No purchase necessary. To enter, follow the directions published. Method of entry may vary. For eligibility, entries must be received no later than March 31, 1996. No liability is assumed for printing errors, lost, late or misdirected entries. Odds of winning are determined by the number of eligible entries distributed and received. Prizewinners will be determined no later than June 30, 1996.

Sweepstakes open to residents of the U.S. (except Puerto Rico), Canada, Europe and Taiwan who are 18 years of age or older. All applicable laws and regulations apply. Sweepstakes offer void wherever prohibited by law. Values of all prizes are in U.S. currency. This sweepstakes is presented by Torstar Corp., its subsidiaries and affiliates, in conjunction with book, merchandise and/or product offerings. For a copy of the Official Rules send a self-addressed, stamped envelope (WA residents need not affix return postage) to: MILLION DOLLAR SWEEPSTAKES (III) Rules, P.O. Box 4573, Blair, NE 68009, USA.

EXTRA BONUS PRIZE DRAWING

No purchase necessary. The Extra Bonus Prize will be awarded in a random drawing to be conducted no later than 5/30/96 from among all entries received. To qualify, entries must be received by 3/31/96 and comply with published directions. Drawing open to residents of the U.S. (except Puerto Rico), Canada, Europe and Taiwan who are 18 years of age or older. All applicable laws and regulations apply; offer void wherever prohibited by law. Odds of winning are dependent upon number of eligibile entries received. Prize is valued in U.S. currency. The offer is presented by Torstar Corp., its subsidiaries and affiliates in conjunction with book, merchandise and/or product offering. For a copy of the Official Rules governing this sweepstakes, send a self-addressed, stamped envelope (WA residents need not affix return postage) to: Extra Bonus Prize Drawing Rules, P.O. Box 4590, Blair, NE 68009, USA.

SWP-S795

He's Too Hot To Handle...but she can take a little heat.

As a Privileged Woman, you'll be entitled to all these Free Benefits. And Free Gifts, too.

To thank you for buying our books, we've designed an exclusive FREE program called *PAGES & PRIVILEGES*™. You can enroll with just one Proof of Purchase, and get the kind of luxuries that, until now, you could only read about.

Big Hotel Discounts

A privileged woman stays in the finest hotels. And so can you—at up to 60% off! Imagine standing in a hotel check-in line and watching as the guest in front of you pays $150 for the same room that's only costing you $60. Your *Pages & Privileges* discounts are good at Sheraton, Marriott, Best Western, Hyatt and thousands of other fine hotels all over the U.S., Canada and Europe.

Free Discount Travel Service

A privileged woman is always jetting to romantic places. When you fly, just make one phone call for the lowest published airfare at time of booking—or double the difference back! PLUS—you'll get a $25 voucher to use the first time you book a flight AND 5% cash back on every ticket you buy thereafter through the travel service!

SD-PP3A

𝓕REE GIFTS!

A privileged woman is always getting wonderful gifts.
Luxuriate in rich fragrances that will stir your senses (and his). This gift-boxed assortment of fine perfumes includes three popular scents, each in a beautiful designer bottle. <u>Truly Lace</u>...This luxurious fragrance unveils your sensuous side. L'Effleur...discover the romance of the Victorian era with this soft floral. <u>Muguet des bois</u>...a single note floral of singular beauty.

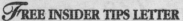

𝓕REE INSIDER TIPS LETTER

A privileged woman is always informed. And you'll be, too, with our free letter full of fascinating information and sneak previews of upcoming books.

𝓜ORE GREAT GIFTS & BENEFITS TO COME

A privileged woman always has a lot to look forward to. And so will you. You get all these wonderful FREE gifts and benefits now with only one purchase...and there are no additional purchases required. However, each additional retail purchase of Harlequin and Silhouette books brings you a step closer to even more great FREE benefits like half-price movie tickets... and even more FREE gifts.

L'Effleur...This basketful of romance lets you discover L'Effleur from head to toe, heart to home.

Truly Lace...
A basket spun with the sensuous luxuries of Truly Lace, including Dusting Powder in a reusable satin and lace covered box.

Complete the Enrollment Form in the front of this book and mail it with this Proof of Purchase.

PROOF OF PURCHASE
Offer expires October 31, 1996

SD-PP3